JOSS

WERE ZOO BOOK NINE

R. E. BUTLER

Joss

Were Zoo Book Nine

By R. E. Butler

JOSS (WERE ZOO BOOK NINE)
BY R. E. BUTLER

This ebook is a work of fiction. Names, characters, places, and incidents are the product of the author's imagination and not to be construed as real. Any resemblance to actual persons, living or dead, events or locations is coincidental.

Disclaimer: The material in this book is for mature audiences only and contains graphic sexual content and is intended for those older than the age of 18 only.

∽

Edited by Evil Eye Editing

Special thanks to photographer Paul Henry Serres for being amazing to work with and to model Eric Trahan, the perfect alpha wolf!

Thanks to Joyce, Shelley, and Ann for beta reading.

JOSS (WERE ZOO BOOK NINE)
BY R. E. BUTLER

All Jeanie Moon has to show for the last twenty-five years of her life is a divorce that left her broke with terrible credit, and a desire to never be in a relationship again. When her twenty-something neighbor gives her a coupon for a free VIP tour at a safari park, she decides there are worse ways to spend a Friday afternoon.

Alpha wolf Joss isn't interested in anything but the Amazing Adventures Safari Park he and his pack call home—that and keeping their shifter abilities a secret from humans. He's happy when one of his males finds a soulmate, but none of his people have found their mate with the help of the VIP tours which were designed to bring in potential mates. When he's called to the tour desk to settle an issue with someone using another person's ticket, he's in for the shock of his life when he discovers his soulmate is the one holding the ticket.

Joss knows that taking a human as his mate means his alphaship is in jeopardy, but he won't give Jeanie up without a fight, even if it means facing off against the one male he never thought he'd see again...his brother.

CHAPTER ONE

Alpha wolf Joss bent his head and took a drink of water from the small pond in the paddock. The pond was shaded by trees, so the water was fairly cool despite the sweltering August temperatures. He hated summer afternoons, his wolf far preferring the frigid temperatures that came with winter. He heard the familiar rumble of an approaching Jeep and gave a short bark to his people who were in their shifts and milling about the paddock.

He headed toward the chain-link fence that enclosed the paddock so that he was closer to the dirt road. Most of the paddocks in the park held shifters—wolves, lions, bears, gorillas, and elephants—who weren't known to humans. Their people worked at the park and lived in an underground city, each group having their own private living space as well as a shared marketplace where food, clothing, and other items were available. Joss had been at the park for nearly thirty years, part of the original group that wanted to create a safe place for their people to live.

Most shifters lived only with their particular group. Wolves would stake out a territory in a small town and keep their shifting identities a secret from the local humans. The were zoo, as he'd come to think of the park, was unique in that there were so many different groups working and living in the same place. The pack was the largest group out of all of them, but they still enjoyed the safety that came from living with others who could watch their backs. Sometimes, Joss longed for the days of his youth when his pack lived in the mountains of Pennsylvania, away from humans, where they could shift at will and didn't have to worry about their secret being revealed.

Those had been the days.

He let out a sigh as the Jeep stopped in front of the paddock, and Jasper, one of his pack members, helped a young female climb from the vehicle. He brought her over to the fence and recited a spiel on wolf facts for her, then took her photo. Jasper looked at the pack through the fence, his eyes questioning.

Was this human any wolf's soulmate?

Joss scented the air, as did his people with him. She smelled like artificial flowers, probably a perfume or body wash of some sort, which was pleasant but didn't stir his beast. Not that he thought he'd ever have a soulmate. He certainly didn't deserve one.

Discreetly shaking his head at Jasper after he took in the disinterested gazes of his pack members, he padded away to the shade and flopped down. Once the Jeep had moved on to the next paddock, he relaxed and closed his eyes, his ears alert for the next Jeep.

Hours later, he sent two of his males to patrol the park in their shift along with two wolves in their human forms, to ensure that no humans were within the park's gates. Once they'd reported back to him that they were clear, he and his people shifted back to human.

Fridays, Saturdays, and Sundays, the shifters who lived in

secret at the Amazing Adventures Safari Park in New Jersey spent time in their shifts for VIP tours. The purpose of the tours was to encourage unmated humans to come to the park, in the hopes that the shifters might recognize their soulmate among the visitors. A soulmate was the one person on the planet meant for a shifter. In Joss's youth, a shifter would never consider a human as a soulmate, not only because their people generally steered clear of them for fear of discovery, but because taking a human soulmate meant removing that person from their life and family to protect the secret. It was an arduous process.

But because so few shifters found their soulmate in other shifters, humans became the more viable option. The alphas of the park got together and created coupons that were sent out to eligible males and females ages eighteen to thirty-five in the tri-state area, offering them free parking and entrance into the park, as well as a ticket for a private tour. The VIP tours had been going on for over a year, and in all that time, only two soulmates had come from them. Two human females who were friends came together, one finding her soulmate in a gorilla, and one in a lion. A panther shifter female had bought a ticket online after being told by another wolf pack that there were shifters at the park. She'd turned out to be the soulmate of an elephant.

"Park's empty, Joss," Alfie called through the fence, drawing Joss from his reverie.

He let out a sharp bark to Alfie who waved and headed back down the path to finish closing up for the night. Then Joss turned to his people and let out a series of sharp barks, letting them know it was safe to shift.

He padded toward the maintenance shed, where one of his people had tugged the large door open so their people could shift inside. Joss let go of his shift and changed forms, letting out a deep sigh as he grabbed his jeans and tugged them on.

"Everything okay?" Ezra asked as he dressed.

"Yes," Joss answered quickly, and then said, "I'm calling a meeting in our private area in ten minutes. Alert the pack members."

"On it," Ezra said, jogging out of the shed and calling to the wolves still milling around.

Joss opened the door located in the floor of the shed and walked down a flight of stairs. At the bottom of the stairs, he entered a code to unlock the door, walked down a hallway, and entered another code. He followed a long hall, passing by the other shifter groups' private areas, and entered another code into the wolves' private area. The big space had painted walls and ceiling to resemble a forest, and what looked like rock-covered dens were actually the façade on the exterior of the small homes. Joss had a home to himself, but many of the unmated males shared a home with two or more friends. There were mated couples within the pack, but most of his people were single.

Including himself.

Not single, technically. He was what humans called a widower. He'd lost his mate to injury during a hunt. Even fifteen years later, he still harbored guilt over what happened to her. She'd been his chosen mate, not his soulmate. A sweet female he'd met at a gathering of packs. They'd decided to have a child together, and the plan had been for her to raise the pup if it was a girl, and him to raise it if it was a boy, but after their son had been born, they'd gotten used to being around each other and decided to mate officially. They'd had a daughter a few years after their son. He'd loved his mate and she'd loved him, but he'd always wondered if them staying together had prevented either of them from finding their true soulmate.

The idealistic young male of his youth was long gone. Hardened by battle and being alpha, and the terrible choices he'd had to make to protect his people.

His mate would certainly hate him if she knew everything he'd done.

Shaking his thoughts away from the darkest place in his mind, he focused on his people coming into their private area. His second-in-command—Brent—stood at his side with his arms folded.

"All accounted for, Alpha," Brent said.

Joss lifted his hand for quiet. "I've gathered everyone tonight to discuss the VIP tours. I know that no wolf has found his or her soulmate through the tours, even though we've been doing them for over a year. I can see that some of you are disheartened. Trust me when I say that all the alphas are. The good news is that the alpha council has sent out another round of VIP tour tickets, and already we've seen an uptick in the number of reservations."

"Do the alphas really believe the tours are going to work? There's hardly any evidence to support it," Ezra, one of the tour drivers, said.

Joss nodded. "They do. I do. Getting unmated males and females into the park is the only way to expose our people to potential mates."

"What about a pack exchange?" Silvanus asked. "Evan just left to hang with another pack. Why can't a few of us do the same—trade off with another pack?"

"That pack has decided not to send anyone to us, so only Evan is going. It was a special circumstance. While it's been done in the past, the alphas feel that switching out members for new ones isn't the way to find soulmates, and I agree. Particularly after what happened with the pack from Rhapsody's town."

There was a murmur of agreement from the pack. Rhapsody was a panther shifter. She'd been told by her aunt before her passing that the wolf pack in their town knew of an entire zoo full of shifters where she could go to find help, as she was the last of her people. The pack had participated in an exchange with Joss's pack at one time with the understanding that they would never tell anyone else about the shifters who lived under the park. Because of their big mouths, a group of panthers had come after Rhapsody and caused a lot of problems.

"I know it's hard to maintain a positive attitude, but we won't be participating in pack exchanges for the foreseeable future. In the meantime, just have faith that we're doing everything we can to help bring people into the park. I fully believe that soulmates will be found eventually, we just have to give it time."

There was a low grumble within the pack, a few of the younger males clearly not agreeing with Joss's stance. But he wasn't in the mood to entertain any backtalk.

With a low snarl, he clapped his hands together and all chatter ceased. "Unless one of you would like to challenge me for alpha?"

He left the words hanging for a little while, staring down the males who'd spoken. Joss wasn't alpha because he'd inherited the position or because he won a popular election. He'd fought his way up the ranks and won the title in battle. He was the alpha because he was the best, period. Eventually he'd step down, or someone would come in who could best him in a fight. But that day hadn't come yet.

When no one would meet his eyes, Joss said, "Then we'll continue to do things as the alphas have decided. Dismissed."

He watched everyone go their separate ways, not speaking until he was standing alone with Brent. As his beta, the second-highest ranked male in the pack, Brent would be the male to beat for alpha when Joss was ready to abdicate.

The previous alpha had been in power well into his sixties. But time marched on for all, and when Joss saw the male was starting to grow weaker, he took the opportunity and challenged for alpha.

He'd beaten the old alpha easily, but since the male had been ready to step down, he'd just needed a nudge.

But then Joss's older brother wanted to be alpha, too.

That battle had not gone well.

Joss had nearly killed his brother because he wouldn't admit defeat. With one foot in the grave, Joss had sent his brother away, exiled forever from the pack and their family.

Of which only Joss remained.

"Alpha?" Brent asked.

"Sorry," Joss said. He was really musing too much today. "What did you say?"

"I said that I haven't heard anyone complaining about the VIP tours outright, but the younger males were pissed that Evan was able to leave when they weren't. I understand it's different circumstances, but you know how the young ones can be."

"It's just not safe for an exchange of any size right now. They'll have to accept that. But if you hear of anyone in particular complaining, let me know."

"Will do. Anything else?"

"No. Have a good night."

"You too."

Joss headed to his home. At one time it had been a haven. Now the solitude he'd once enjoyed mocked him.

All alone. No family. No one who loved him. No one he could love.

The guilt within him flared as he thought about love. He certainly wasn't a male who deserved the love of anyone, let alone his soulmate. He'd had love and lost it. He'd had children and they were gone. Everything he'd had at one point in his life that had given him joy was gone. He didn't believe there was a female on the planet who'd forgive him for what he'd done in the name of protecting the pack. Destined to be alone, he was sure, for the rest of his life, he went to the kitchen and pulled out a glass, pouring himself a shot of whiskey. He could dull his mind enough so he could rest.

That was the most he could hope for.

CHAPTER TWO

Jeanie Moon set a plate of eggs, home fries, and sausage links on the metal counter and clapped the bell with the handle of the spatula. "Regina, order up."

"Thanks," the middle-aged woman said as she looked at the ticket and plate. "When you have a sec, can you make me an English muffin? I'm starving."

"Sure thing," Jeanie said, smiling.

Turning her attention to the row of orders, she busied herself at the cooktop making breakfast for the locals. Friday mornings were busy, the farmers coming in after they'd done their morning chores, eager for hearty breakfasts and strong coffee. She could practically make the regulars' orders by memory after working at the diner for the last two years.

It wasn't what she'd thought she'd be doing at age forty-four, but life had a way of making a fool of anyone with a plan. She'd gone to college for finance and had worked her way up in the corporate world. Then the business had closed its doors right at the time she'd discovered her husband was cheating on her and had been doing it for a long time. He'd butt-dialed her while she was at an interview, and the video call had shown her a lot more than she'd ever wanted to see of her husband and another woman rolling around in bed together.

She'd filed for divorce, and discovered that he'd mortgaged the house twice, and after she left him, he got revenge on her by taking out credit cards in her name and maxing them out. Once her credit tanked, she'd been unable to find a job in the finance world. She was seen as a bad risk because she couldn't handle her own finances.

Desperate for work, she'd taken a job as a waitress at Ron's Diner, the pitiful hourly wage and small checks not even allowing her to cover the mortgage of the house. Ron had taken pity on her and put her behind the stove instead. She'd never cooked for more than a couple people before, but the menu was simple, and she'd grown into the role. Now, she enjoyed it. And she'd even helped Ron with his accounting and saved him some money on his taxes. It was the least she could do since he gave her a chance when she'd had no experience.

She popped an English muffin into one of the many-slotted toasters on the counter and put a little plate in front of it, then turned her attention to the omelet she needed to make for the next order. The morning zipped by quickly, and once she'd finished up the lunch rush, she clocked out and said goodbye to Ron and Regina.

"You have plans tonight?" Regina asked, leaning against the front counter and snapping her gum.

"Oh yeah, hot date with my television and new sci-fi series that's streaming on one of the services."

"Sounds dreamy," Regina said with a laugh. "I can fix you up with someone. My cousin Dell is a truck driver, so he's only home on weekends."

"That's a selling point?" she asked with a laugh.

"Well, if you like your space, yeah."

Jeanie shook her head at her friend. "Thanks anyway, I'm good. This time I'm going to wait for Mr. Right to sweep me off my feet, and I'm not going to rush into anything."

"Good for you."

Saying goodbye until her shift on Sunday morning, Jeanie got in her car and drove to the split double she rented. On the other side was a young woman named Glennis, who'd been on vacation for the last week and had asked Jeanie to feed her temperamental Persian, Mr. Pickles. She pulled into the driveway and parked, smiling when she saw Glennis waving at her from the open door.

"You weren't supposed to be back until tomorrow. How was your vacation?" Jeanie hugged her.

"Great. We had a chance to take an earlier flight, so we figured why not. How was Mr. P?"

"Sassy as ever."

"I have a surprise for you, come on in."

Jeanie walked into the other side of the split house and shut the screen door so the wily cat didn't escape.

"How was work?" Glennis asked as she busied herself at the kitchen table.

"Same old, same old. Did you do anything extra fun on vacation or just hang out on the beach?"

"Just the beach. We did eat at some great restaurants, though. Oh, here it is!" Glennis turned around and handed Jeanie a small gift bag.

"You didn't have to get me anything," she said as she took the bag.

"I know, but you're my friend and you did me a huge favor taking care of Sir Sassy Pants." Glennis smiled at her cat who was sitting with his back to her on the couch.

Jeanie opened the little bag and pulled out an envelope and a clear cellophane bag of salt water taffy. "My favorite!"

"I remembered. And I only got the fruit ones, because you said you liked those best."

Inside the envelope was a ticket for a free safari tour at Amazing Adventures Safari Park.

Glennis put her hand on Jeanie's. "Now don't go thinking I'm super wonderful for getting you the tour ticket, it came in the mail to me and I can't use it because I work when the tour is, and I can't take off any more time for something like that. Even if it does sound fun. So you can use the ticket on my behalf."

Jeanie looked at the ticket for a moment, tempted to tell her no thanks.

"Don't say no," Glennis said.

Jeanie looked at her. "I was thinking about it, but it might actually be fun. I've never been to the park or on any kind of safari tour."

"I went when I was a kid, it was fun. But this is a private tour. Free parking, free admittance to the park, and you book your tour time online, Friday, Saturday, or Sunday."

Jeanie hummed. "I'll do it."

"Take lots of pics."

"I will." She gave the young lady a cheek kiss and thanked her again for the gifts, then headed home.

She had a date with a big bowl of popcorn and a new sci-fi show, and then she'd maybe see about booking the private safari tour. Who knew what adventure might be waiting for her?

CHAPTER THREE

J eanie handed her ticket to a woman at the park entrance and placed her sunglasses on her head.

"Welcome," the woman said with a smile. "Do you know where you're going?"

"No."

The woman opened a park map and ran her finger along one of the pathways. "It's through the gates and to the left. Stop at the ticket booth, tell them your reservation time, and they'll take it from there."

"Great, thanks."

"Have fun!"

Jeanie took back her ticket and the map, and walked into the park. She couldn't believe she'd never been to the park. There were certainly parks around New Jersey, but both her parents worked when she was growing up and weekends had been for working around the house. In high school, she'd gone on a class trip to the aquarium, but that wasn't quite the same as an actual zoo.

Humming a tune, she followed the path to the ticket booth, where there were two young men wearing blue park uniforms. They smiled at her when she walked up to the booth and laid the ticket down.

"I'm here for my three o'clock reservation."

"Welcome," one whose name tag read Jasper said. "I just need your ID."

She took her ID out of her wristlet and handed it over.

Jasper frowned, tilting the ID and ticket toward the other man, whose nametag read Greg.

"Your ID and ticket don't match."

"My neighbor gave me her ticket. It doesn't say on the ticket that it's not transferable." She'd double-checked when she made the reservation, and there was nowhere on the ticket or the park website that said one person couldn't gift another person the ticket.

"But it's not your name," Greg said, his brows lowering.

"And?"

"Hold on, we need to call our boss," Greg said.

He and Jasper stepped away from the booth, and Jeanie felt her cheeks heat with embarrassment. She didn't like being put on the spot. Fortunately there was no one around but the two young men; still, she was uncomfortable.

And then she overheard it.

"She's too old," Greg whispered, not quietly enough for her not to pick up what he said.

"I know, I know," Jasper said, sighing.

Jeanie's mouth fell open and she sucked in a sharp breath. Her cheeks heated further as mortification filled her. She was only forty-four, hardly old by any stretch. She blinked away the tears that surged, angry at herself for being embarrassed by two kids who didn't know how to properly whisper.

"I'll call the boss," Jasper said.

Greg turned to Jeanie with a tight smile. "It'll just be a sec."

She nodded, not trusting herself to speak. She fully wanted to crawl in a hole and never show her face again.

~

Joss grunted in annoyance as he headed up to the safari tour booth. He wasn't really irritated by the issue at the booth—someone using someone else's ticket—it was that his wolf had been bugging the hell out of him all morning. He'd gone for a run in his shift early in the morning, pacing the entire paddock several times in an attempt to wear out his beast—but it had done nothing but agitate the creature. He'd never felt so on edge, and he couldn't figure out why.

And then, as he'd been trying to focus on a spreadsheet detailing the operational costs of the tours for the third quarter, he'd gotten a damn call about the safari.

The tickets had been sent out to eligible males and females between the ages of eighteen and thirty-five. It didn't matter to him that the female who came in with someone else's ticket was over the age; it wasn't a hard limit as far as he knew. But Jasper and Greg weren't wrong—the tickets weren't intended for use by anyone but the person they were mailed to. The fact the tickets didn't have printed on them that they weren't to be shared was something the alphas and marketing team had overlooked.

He'd been tempted to tell the males to just let her on the damn tour because there wasn't any harm in it, aside from the fact that it was possible the female intended for the tour actually was someone's soulmate. For some damn reason, his wolf demanded he go to the tour booth and handle it in person.

As he strode swiftly to the booth, he first saw her long, dark hair. It fell past her shoulders in thick, chocolate waves with little highlights of caramel and red in the strands. She was wearing jean shorts with embroidered flowers on the pockets, and a red short-sleeved shirt. His wolf went quiet within him, an intense connection between himself and the woman blooming immediately.

It wasn't possible, was it?

Had a transferred ticket brought Joss his soulmate?

Swallowing against the sudden lump in his throat, he stopped next to the female, inhaling her scent. She smelled like coconut, a scent he'd never cared for before but suddenly was his favorite. She turned and looked up at him, her hazel eyes luminous with unshed tears.

"Did you come to send me home for being too old?" she whispered harshly, her kissable mouth turned down in a frown.

He wanted to reach out and comfort her, but she was human and humans didn't necessarily understand a mate connection. Hell, Joss wasn't sure he believed it himself until this very moment.

"Absolutely not." His mind raced, his wolf not wanting anyone else near her. "I came to take you on the tour myself."

Her brows winged up. "What?"

"If you're too old for this, then I am. I'm forty-seven, and the boss. I'm going to encourage my employees to apologize for being assholes, and then I'm going to take you for a tour." He glanced at Jasper and Greg, who were staring at him with mouths open and eyes wide. He let out a short growl that he knew to her ears would sound like a grunt. The males snapped into movement.

"We're really sorry," Jasper said. "We were rude, it's not acceptable."

"Sorry," Greg said. "We didn't mean to offend you."

"It's okay," she said.

Jasper handed her back her ticket and ID.

"I'm Joss," he said, offering his hand after she'd put her things away.

She took it, an electric jolt racing up his arm at the contact. "I'm Jeanie. I really didn't mean to cause any trouble."

"You didn't, I promise. Let's head down to the jeeps."

"Joss, there are people waiting," Greg said, his voice a submissive murmur.

"And?" Joss looked hard at the young male, who turned his head down and tilted it, showing deference to his alpha.

"Nothing. Sorry."

"Come on, Jeanie."

Joss took her to the front of the tour where four females were waiting. He told Jeanie to wait and walked over to the next jeep idling near the waiting females.

Silvanus gave Joss a curious look when he walked over to him. "Hey," he said. "What's up?"

"I'm going to take this jeep out myself," he said. "For a private tour."

The young male hesitated. "We... you do know there are people waiting?"

Joss didn't say anything; he simply waited for Silvanus to realize he was contradicting his alpha. It was almost comical when the realization occurred to Silvanus, because his eyes went really wide and then he scrambled out of the jeep. "Sorry, sorry," he murmured, his voice low and his head tilted to the side.

Joss nodded. "If anyone asks, tell them that she missed her time slot and we wanted to fit her in. Be sure to offer those waiting a chilled bottle of water—it's hot as hell out here."

Silvanus nodded enthusiastically. Joss returned to Jeanie and brought her to the Jeep, helping her to climb into the passenger seat. Normally, two wolves went on the tour—a driver and a guide—with the human sitting in the back seat.

But he didn't need or want a guide with him, not only because he'd helped draft the script the guides used to talk about the animals, but because he wasn't sure how his wolf would handle another unmated male so close to his newly-found soulmate.

Pulling the jeep up to the entrance of the tour, he idled, waiting until the first paddock was clear. He nodded to Brent who was part of the tour's security team, who then pressed the button to open the gate. It creaked as it opened, and Joss drove through, waiting until it was fully closed before he continued on.

"So," Joss said, "have you ever been to the park before?"

"No," Jeanie said, tucking a lock of hair behind her ear. She gave him a tentative smile when he looked at her, and it warmed his whole body. Damn she was beautiful.

"I've been here for thirty years."

"I take it you don't always drive people on tours?"

"No. I oversee the tours and work in the finance department. What do you do for a living?"

"I'm a cook at a diner in Barreston."

"Do you enjoy it?" He pulled to a stop in front of the wolf paddock.

She hummed and looked toward the fence. "I love cooking, but I went to college for finance. I just can't... work in that field anymore."

He didn't care for the way her voice lowered in defeat, as if someone had purposely caused her to not be able to work where she wanted to. She folded her arms over her chest, and he got the distinct impression she didn't want to share any more about work with him. While part of him wanted to know everything about her immediately, he couldn't order her to tell him. She was human. And he was trying not to be an ass.

"Let's go see the wolves." He put the jeep in park and got

out, jogging around to help her. He grabbed the camera from the bag in the seat next to her and walked her to the fence. He told her a little about the wolves and was happy when she seemed to relax, finally rewarding him with a smile when he told her he was going to take a picture of her at each paddock for the keepsake photo album she'd be presented with before she left the park.

"I didn't get you in trouble, did I?" she asked after she smiled for the photo and then turned back to the paddock.

"Of course not. The perk of being the boss is I get to help out lovely ladies when they need it."

She chuckled. "I'm sure they're all very grateful to be rescued by a handsome guy like you."

His wolf was practically prancing in his mind like a show horse at her praise.

"To be honest, you're my first rescue. How am I doing?"

"Really well."

He grinned and led her back to the jeep, where they continued on to the next paddock once the vehicle ahead of them had moved on. He radioed to the security team that he was finished at the first paddock. "Why do you have to wait for the other jeep?"

"It's a private tour," he said. "We don't want to encroach on anyone else's time."

"Has it always been a private tour? I don't remember ever seeing a commercial on TV for it or hearing about it."

He explained that until about a year ago, they hadn't had the private tours, but had decided sending out coupons for them would be a good way to bring people back into the park. "A lot of people say they came to the park when they were young, but not as adults. We wanted to remind people that we're here."

The tour was over all too quickly, even though he'd done his best to stall for time. He wanted her to stay with him as long as possible, but he didn't want to come on too strongly. He parked in line at the start of the tour and grabbed the SD card from the camera. His mind raced as she got out of the vehicle, tugged on her shorts, and gave him a curious smile.

"Thanks for the tour, Joss. I really enjoyed it."

His wolf howled. *Don't let her go!*

"It will take an hour for the photo album to be ready. Would you like some company? We can get something to eat."

She looked at him, tilting her head as she seemed to study him. "I'm not upset about what happened with the ticket. I mean, I was fully mortified when I overheard them say I was too old, and I still don't understand why there's an age limit on the private tours. But your workers were just doing what they're told. You don't have to babysit me or go to any extreme lengths to try to make me happy. I won't sue the park or anything."

He let out an aggravated sigh. He wanted to beat those two males within an inch of their lives for making Jeanie feel bad. She wasn't old, she was perfect.

Perfect for him.

If he could only figure out what to do next.

The question was, how could an alpha wolf who didn't believe he even deserved a soulmate go about romancing the alluring human before him?

Jeanie thought Joss was the sexiest guy she'd ever met. Tall, broad shouldered, wearing a golf shirt that stretched tight along his muscular upper body. His hair was dark blond, his short-trimmed beard sprinkled with gray that only enhanced the sexiness. Why was it women had to dye every last gray hair but men could let it go and looked sexy as hell?

His left arm was covered with tattoos that disappeared up under the sleeve of his shirt. She had a tattoo herself, a small Monarch butterfly on her ankle. She'd gotten it when her divorce was finalized, and she was finally able to start a new chapter of her life. It seemed a fitting way to mark her transformation. Certainly, she wasn't who she thought she'd be at this point in her life, but she liked who she was now. She had friends and a good job that she didn't hate most of the time, and in general she was happy.

"I'm not being nice because my people insulted you," Joss said, drawing her attention from the tattoos on his arm to his face.

"So why are you being nice, then? I don't think that it's normal for VIP tour drivers to spend a few hours walking around with their passenger."

"It's not. But let's just say that I'm not ready to say goodbye to you yet. If that's okay with you."

She pursed her lips to hide the grin that wanted to break free. He wanted to spend time with her? Holy crap!

"I'm not ready to say goodbye, either."

He smiled and it made her stomach flutter.

Since she'd never been to the park, he took her on an official tour, taking her to every exhibit including a bird sanctuary that would be opening in the future. They finished the tour at a food stall that served baskets of fried chicken strips and french fries. They found an empty picnic table under the shade of a tree and sat across from each other.

"What's your favorite food?" she asked, cutting a piece of chicken and dunking it into a plastic container of honey mustard.

"Steak. You?"

"Mac and cheese. I make mac and cheese at the diner when I work the dinner shift, but Ron the owner only likes the classic style, not anything fun or different."

"Like what?" Joss asked.

"Well, I was at a drive-in restaurant a few months ago and they had mac and cheese topped with barbecue brisket and onion rings. And once I ate at a fancy restaurant in Philly and had lobster mac and cheese, which was fabulous. I always thought it would be neat to have a food truck that only served mac and cheese."

"Why don't you do that?"

"Money."

He nodded in understanding. "They're pretty expensive to get up and running. But if you'd ever like to make fun mac and cheese, I'd be happy to be your taste tester."

"Oh?"

"Of course."

She smiled and looked down at her food, stabbing another piece of chicken. "Do you live around here?"

"I do. You?"

"I live in Barreston, so only about forty minutes away. I moved into a rental house after I..." She paused, not wanting to lay her whole crappy history on him before they even made plans for an actual date.

His eyes narrowed slightly, and he put his fork down and reached across the table to take her hand. She felt a zing of pleasure shoot up her arm at the warm, firm pressure of his grip. "You don't have to tell me anything you don't want to, Jeanie, but whatever you do tell me, I promise won't garner any judgement from me. We've all got a past. Whatever happened in your life before today brought you here to the park so that you and I could meet."

She squeezed his hand back, then launched into the tale of her adult life that left her at this point—working at a greasy spoon with a mountain of bad debt from her asshole ex, with no kids or family left.

He made a sound that reminded her a lot of an angry

growl, and she swore his eyes changed color to a dark amber. But it was surely a trick of the sunlight streaming through the trees.

"I was... married," he said. "She passed away fifteen years ago from an infection from an injury. My daughter died when she fell from a tree when she was little, and then my son died." His voice faltered, and his eyes got so sad looking. He cleared his throat. "Now it's just me. The workers at the zoo are like my family now, but it's not quite the same as having someone that's just mine, you know?"

Nodding, she said, "Yeah. I totally get that."

His phone buzzed on the picnic table, and he turned the screen over. "Your album is ready. Would you like to get some ice cream on the way? There's a stall that's got some pretty amazing flavors."

"I'd love to."

They threw away their trash and walked to an ice cream stall where a man and woman were handing out cones to kids that were decorated with cookies and candies to make them look like bears.

"Hey, Tayme," Joss said, coming up to the side of the stall. "This is my friend, Jeanie. This is Tayme and his wife, Rory."

"Nice to meet you," Rory said, shaking Jeanie's hand.

"What can we get for you?" Tayme asked.

Jeanie looked at the flavors. "Oh, mint chip. I love that."

"Make it two," Joss said.

Rory scooped the pale green ice cream dotted with chocolate chunks into freshly made sugar cones and handed them over. "Enjoy."

Joss thanked them for the ice cream, and he and Jeanie walked and talked, meandering down one path and then another. By the time their cones were gone, they'd reached a gift shop. Inside the air-conditioned store, she smiled as she saw the shelves of stuffed animals. They had every animal on the tour, from a moose that was nicknamed Tank to the huge elephants and dozens of wolves.

"Here you go," Joss said, taking the photo album from a woman behind the counter.

"Thanks," Jeanie said, flipping through a few of the pages. "You're a pretty good photographer."

"I had a lovely subject."

She smiled. "You're sweet."

He cleared his throat. "I hate to have to say goodbye, but I need to get back to the office. Don't feel obligated to leave, you should stay and enjoy the park as long as you'd like."

"I think I'm ready to go home."

"I'll walk you to your car."

"You don't have to."

"But I want to."

"Okay." Tucking the album under her arm, she walked with Joss out of the store and to the front gate. She had to get her phone and look for the photo she'd taken of the row number where she'd parked. Once she was standing next to her old car, she smiled up at Joss. She wasn't a really forward person. She'd never asked a guy out before, but she was certain if she drove off without at least asking for his number, she'd regret it for the rest of her life.

"I'd like to ask you out," Joss blurted out suddenly.

"Oh! You would? I was just thinking about asking you myself. I'd love to see you again. Give me your phone and I'll put my number in it."

He unlocked his phone and she created a new contact, adding her name, phone number, and address.

"I could pick you up for dinner tomorrow night," he said, taking back his phone.

"Seven?" she offered.

He nodded, looking at the screen and smiling. Her phone buzzed and she saw a text from him that said, "It's me, Joss."

"Seven's perfect. Do you have a food preference?" he asked.

"Anything but a diner."

He chuckled. "I'll choose a great place."

For a moment, they just stared at each other, his gaze flickering from her eyes to her lips. She thought he might kiss her, and she was fully prepared to let him. But he just smiled and opened her car door for her.

"Until tomorrow, Jeanie," he said, his voice dropping a little lower and making things deep within her cheer.

"Bye, Joss."

He shut the door and she turned on the car, then backed out of the parking spot. She waved and he waved back, and she swore she saw his eyes turn amber once more.

Another trick of the sun, she was sure.

Once she was on her way home, she turned on the radio and put the windows down. She couldn't believe how her day had turned out, and it was all thanks to Glennis's VIP tour ticket, and a sexy guy named Joss who came to her rescue.

CHAPTER FOUR

Joss didn't sleep well Saturday night. His wolf wanted to go to Jeanie's house and just watch over her. His human side knew he couldn't do that. It would be akin to stalking, and certainly not the way he wanted to start things off with his soulmate.

Soulmate.

The word made his heart clench.

What would she think of him when he told her everything?

Not just that he was a shifter, which her kind didn't know anything about. But that he'd killed his own son in the name of protecting that secret.

As an alpha, he'd learned to never show fear, under any circumstance. Even though his people had no issue with him as alpha, there were pack members who watched him closely for signs of weakness. He didn't want to stop being alpha until he was good and ready. So he couldn't go to any of his people and ask for advice on dating. They'd see his unease with the situation and potentially think him in need of being taken out of power.

So he'd have to find someone else to talk to about dating.

He wanted to romance Jeanie, but he had zero idea how to do it.

It would be far easier if she were a shifter. Then she'd feel the soulmate connection between them. As it stood, he couldn't reveal his shifting nature to her until she was in love with him.

How the hell long would that even take?

His wolf was already half in love with her. Every time he thought of her his beast wanted to roll onto his back for some belly rubs, which was fully out of character for the predator in him.

His mind flitted to a human male who worked in the finance department. Devlin was mated to Jenni, a lioness. Making a mental note to speak to Devlin about romancing a human, he closed his eyes and ordered his wolf to settle down. In less than twenty-four hours he'd be seeing Jeanie again, and they could start the process of winning her heart. He could think of nothing better than waking up for the rest of his life with the dark-haired beauty in his arms.

Later that morning, Devlin knocked on Joss's office door. "You left a message you wanted to see me?"

"Come in. Shut the door."

Devlin did as requested and sat in one of the chairs across the desk from Joss. "I feel a bit like a kid getting called to the principal's office."

Joss chuckled. "Nothing bad, I promise. I do need to ask for your discretion."

"Of course. Whatever you say is just between us."

Joss explained how he'd come to meet Jeanie.

Devlin's brows arched. "No kidding? That's great! Congratulations."

"Thank you," Joss said. "I have a date with her tonight, but I'm at an utter loss. I have no idea how to romance a human female. I've spent my whole life almost entirely surrounded by shifters."

Devlin nodded. "Jenni says it's easier to deal with shifters because they don't have the hang ups that humans do. Like waiting until you're in love with someone before you get married. How can I help?"

"What can you tell me about human women? What will she expect from me?"

"Well, they're all different of course. Be a gentleman—get the door for her, bring her flowers, pay for dinner."

"Flowers?"

"Sure. Roses are a good bet, a dozen should do the trick. Be sure to compliment her, too. Women love that. Jenni gets all flustered and adorable when I tell her that kind of stuff."

"How long will it take to get her to love me?"

Devlin's brows nearly disappeared into his hairline. "Shit, Joss. You can't plan that sort of thing. Some humans fall in love fast, some don't. Depending on how much baggage she's got from her ex, she may be wary of jumping into a relationship. Since you can't tell her about your shift until she's in love with you, she may pick up on the fact you're holding something back from her. I knew there was something different about Jenni before she told me. It's like there's a part of her that she kept from me, and it made me nuts."

Joss's wolf didn't like hearing they couldn't put a timeline together for moving things forward with Jeanie.

"You could always go the route of bringing her in and shifting for her before she loves you. Of course, that has its own problems with it."

Joss nodded. One of the human mates had been brought

to a meeting room and her soulmate had shifted in front of her. The alphas had made it clear, however, that if they went through with the shift that she wouldn't be allowed to leave the park until it was certain that she wouldn't betray them. It was too risky a move for now.

"Thanks for the advice," Joss said.

"Where does she live?"

"Barreston."

"I know a great steakhouse not too far from there. I can make a reservation for the two of you if you'd like."

"Thanks. That would be great. Seven thirty?"

"Perfect. I'll text you the details. And good luck."

Joss nodded. When he was alone in his office, he attempted to get some work done, but now his wolf was too excited by the prospect of seeing her in a few hours. He decided it would be better to just cut his losses and go to the marketplace underneath the zoo and see if he could find something to wear on his date.

Two of his wolves—Zeger and his mate, Anke—worked in the marketplace, a central location where their people could get food prepared by the bear shifters, clothing and other items from the wolves, and females could get their nails painted by two of the human soulmates.

"Hello Alpha," Anke said when Joss walked up to the counter.

"I'm in need of dress clothes."

"Of course. We've got a nice selection of slacks, shirts, and shoes." She led him toward the back of the shop where several racks held different sizes of clothing. He chose black dress pants and a gray dress shirt, picking out a tie that had gray and olive tones mixed together, the green shades reminding him of Jeanie's hazel eyes. Once he'd gathered his clothes for his date, he thanked Anke and headed to his house to get ready. He still had several hours ahead of him before he needed to leave, but he couldn't sit around in the office anymore. His wolf was restless and excited to see Jeanie.

He trimmed his beard, showered, and got dressed once it drew closer to the time he needed to leave. Topside, he checked out an unmarked SUV. The park used marked SUVs for zoo business and unmarked ones for private business. They'd had a problem in the past with people following the marked vehicles back to the zoo.

Setting the GPS to Jeanie's address, he sent her a text to say he was on the way. When she responded quickly that she was looking forward to seeing him, his wolf started doing cartwheels in his head. Shaking his head at himself and his crazy wolf, he left the park and headed to her place to go on his first-ever date. With a human.

Who happened to be his soulmate.

CHAPTER FIVE

Jeanie looked at her closet and sighed deeply. Standing in her bedroom still wearing her favorite fluffy robe, she simply couldn't decide what to wear. It was a first date, but somehow it felt even more important than that. She couldn't put her finger on why it felt so monumental. It wasn't as if she hadn't dated since her divorce. She'd been on a few blind dates, had gone to a local bar with Regina a time or two, but no one had warranted more than a second date at the most, and often the first date was plenty.

She picked up her phone and video called Glennis.

"Hey neighbor," Glennis said.

"I need help. I have a date. He's going to be here in like an hour, and I don't know what to wear."

"Oh! I'd love to help. I'll be right over."

"Thanks, you're a life saver."

The call ended, and a few minutes later, Glennis was standing in front of Jeanie's closet, swishing the hangers back and forth on the metal rod as she looked through her clothes.

"I've never been to Jacquard's," Glennis said. "Do you know how fancy it is?"

Jeanie had never been to it either, but after Joss told her he'd made reservations for dinner, she'd checked out their website and seen what appeared to be a fairly upscale restaurant. "Pretty fancy, I think."

Glennis hummed a little tune, off-key, and dug way into the back of Jeanie's closet.

"Ah-ha," Glennis said as she emerged with a short skirt and a fitted blouse that Jeanie hadn't seen in years.

"Um, the skirt's kind of short."

"Yeah, and? Come on, you've got a great figure. You hide it behind loose stuff, show off those curves!"

Jeanie made a face but couldn't stop from smiling at her infectious tone. "I'll try them."

"What's your undies situation?"

"What?"

"You should always wear sexy undies on dates."

While she certainly had entertained some fantasies about the all-too-sexy Joss, she didn't plan on getting naked that night. "He's not going to see anything but these clothes on my body."

Glennis rolled her eyes. "Oh, please, I don't mean you need to give away the farm, or whatever the saying is. Confidence starts with sexy undies. You'll feel sexy just knowing you have them on, and that'll come across to him. Guys like a confident woman."

"Okay, I'll give it a try."

She found her sexiest matching bra and panty set—a pink floral satin and lace set she'd splurged on after the divorce was finalized. She'd never worn them, though. But she would tonight. For Joss.

Heading into the bathroom, she dressed in the short navy skirt and put on the elbow-length fitted top. She'd left her hair loose and long, the wavy strands cascading past her shoulders. She applied her makeup—which she'd learned from watching a few online videos, since she normally didn't do more than the bare minimum.

"Come on, lemme see!" Glennis said.

Inhaling, Jeanie opened the bathroom door and stepped out.

"Oh, you look so great!"

Jeanie slipped into a pair of low heels and put a few beaded bracelets on her wrist, then looked at herself in the mirror.

"What do you think?" Glennis asked, coming to stand with her. "I think he's going to lose his shit when he sees you."

Jeanie wanted to look special for Joss. Wanted the date to go well.

"Thank you so much, you picked out a perfect outfit."

She hugged the younger woman.

"Anytime. Text me and let me know how the night goes. Good luck!"

Jeanie walked Glennis to the front door and closed it behind her, looking at her watch and seeing that the time was close to when he was due. She paced from the kitchen to the family room and back, her nerves not letting her sit for long. She heard a vehicle pull into the driveway, and her heart started to pound as anticipation rolled through her.

Calm down, she chided herself. *You don't want to look desperate.*

There was a knock at the door and her mouth went dry. Smoothing her trembling hands down the skirt to straighten it, she took in a few calming breaths to settle her flying pulse and opened the door.

Joss looked amazing, from the top of his carefully styled hair to the shiny black dress shoes on his feet.

"You look beautiful," Joss said, his eyes wide and his voice filled with awe.

He was standing on the tiny front porch holding a bouquet of red roses. And staring at her.

"Are those for me?" she prompted.

He jolted out of his reverie. "Ah, yes. I hope you like them."

"I do, they're lovely, thank you. Come on in, I'll put these in water before we go."

She smiled when she turned away from him, liking that he was as nervous to see her as she'd been to see him. She found a vase in the cupboard, removed the wrapping from the stems, and put them in the vase, giving it a bit of water.

Carrying the vase out to the family room, she put it on the coffee table and smiled at Joss. "Thank you."

"My pleasure." His voice was low and gruff, and she liked it. "Are you ready to go?"

"Absolutely."

The meal was perfect. Hell, everything about their first date was perfect. He'd brought her flowers, acted like a total gentleman, and spent the evening listening to her talk about herself. Whenever she tried to steer the conversation to him, he would give a short answer and then ask her something about herself. Joss was a mystery, and she was pretty sure he was keeping something back. She didn't think it was terrible, but there was definitely something he wasn't telling her.

She didn't let it bother her, though. She had a feeling that he'd tell her more about himself as they got to know each other. She did feel like she'd known him for a lot longer than a day, though. By the time the date was over, she was one hundred percent crazy about him, and while she wanted to put the brakes on her imagination and crazy fantasies, she didn't mind it one bit when they were settled in his comfortable SUV and he took one of her hands and set it on his thigh.

"That may be the best steak I've ever had," Joss said.

"Me, too. Thank you so much for dinner."

"I'm glad you could join me."

They rode in comfortable silence to her house. The moment that he put the SUV into park, her heart kicked up a few notches. Before the date, she'd been very firm about her intentions to let the date end without anything sexy happening. But now that she'd spent a few hours with him—this sexy, intoxicating man—she absolutely didn't want it to be over. She wasn't sure what to say, didn't trust herself not to just blurt out how much she wanted to be with him, so she said nothing.

Joss unbuckled his seatbelt and turned in the seat, resting his arm over the steering wheel. He looked out the windshield toward the house which was illuminated by the headlights.

They both spoke at the same time. She said his name, he said hers. Then they laughed.

"You go first, sweetheart," Joss said, giving her hand a squeeze.

She'd spent the evening being honest with him. She'd laid all her past bare before him and held nothing back. She wasn't about to start lying now.

"Would you like to come in?"

He cleared his throat and she thought once more that she'd seen his eyes flash to a different color. "More than anything, Jeanie, but I can't."

Her heart clenched and disappointment washed over her. "Oh, okay."

Cupping her face, he said, "Don't think for a second that I don't want to. Because all I've been thinking about since we met yesterday was how much I want to be with you. But I'm not looking for a fling or a one-nighter, and I don't think you are, either."

"No."

"I don't trust myself to get you alone and not wind up in bed, and I don't want you to think I'm only interested in that." He leaned in and brushed his lips lightly over hers.

If it was possible, she fell in love with him right then.

Sexy, wonderful man.

She leaned into him and kissed him, unbuckling her seatbelt and moving as close as she could with the console between them. He tilted her head and deepened the kiss, sliding his tongue expertly along hers and making shivers race down her spine. Her whole body was on fire, her skin tingling and her head spinning when the kiss ended far too soon.

He got out of the SUV and came around to her side, opening her door and helping her out. She was simultaneously disappointed and elated. He wasn't looking for a quick roll in the hay, and while she was certain that nothing would be better than that, she wanted more, too. She wanted everything with Joss.

Keys in hand, she unlocked the front door and then looked up at him.

"Call me when you're done with your shift tomorrow," Joss said.

"I will."

He glanced at the door and she caught a hint of his cologne—it was the sexiest smell ever. It reminded her of the woods in fall.

Turning his gaze back to her, he said, "I had a great time tonight, Jeanie. You're amazing, and I'm so glad you took your friend's ticket and came to the park so we could meet."

"Me too."

He kissed her lightly and took a step away. "Good night, sweetheart."

"Good night, Joss."

She swore as he walked down the sidewalk that she heard a growl, but she shook her head thinking that like the many times she thought she'd seen his eyes change color, her mind was playing tricks on her. Joss didn't have color-changing eyes, and she didn't just hear him growl like a beast.

She was pretty sure, anyway.

CHAPTER SIX

Joss was the most miserable he'd ever been in his life. Not taking Jeanie up on her invitation to come into her house on Sunday night had been difficult. He'd been arguing with his wolf all night. He wanted Jeanie to know that he wasn't trying to rush things physically because he didn't want her to think he was just looking for sex. He told himself that waiting until she was ready would be worth it, because he didn't just want her body in his bed, he wanted her heart, too.

His wolf had tried to convince him that they could have both, but Joss managed to walk away from his mate without doing more than kissing. His wolf had been pissed. Hell, he was still pissed.

But he and Jeanie had spent the last week video chatting every day after she finished work. They texted periodically during the day, and she always seemed to know just when he needed a little note from her.

He strode down the hall to the meeting room underneath the park. He'd called a council meeting, where each alpha and his right-hand male would come together to discuss important matters. It had been a week since he'd met Jeanie, and he was quickly losing the battle to keep all of his secrets to himself. It was fast, but he was in love with her, and he wanted to bring her to the park and show her his shift.

Brent was waiting at the door to the meeting room.

"Everything okay?" Brent asked.

"Yes."

"Okay, it's just that you haven't called an alpha meeting before when things were just fine. I feel like you've been a hundred miles away this week. And I'm not the only one who noticed."

Joss stared at his number-two. He hadn't tried to hide anything from his people, but he also hadn't told anyone about meeting her. "I'll explain everything."

Brent nodded sharply and walked into the meeting room ahead of Joss. The alphas were seated around the long table—Marcus the bear alpha, Atticus the gorilla alpha, Caesar the lion alpha, and Alistair the elephant alpha. Their second-in-command males were standing behind them. Joss nodded at everyone and took his seat, gesturing for Jupiter, Caesar's number-two, to shut the door.

"Thank you all for coming," Joss said. "As you know, we had an issue last week on the VIP tour with someone giving their ticket away."

Joss had written a report about the situation to let the alphas know what occurred.

"We're certain this hasn't happened before?" Atticus asked.

"Yes," Joss said. "The ticket-takers have always checked IDs against the tickets, and until last weekend, they've always matched."

"But you allowed her to go on the tour anyway," Caesar said.

"Right. While she was over the age limit we'd set in place

for the tour, I took her on it myself. And that reason is why I wanted to speak to you all today." He paused and looked around at the alphas. They were his friends and the males he came to when he needed advice. The alphas were always there for each other, and he trusted they'd be there for him today, too. "The human who took her friend's ticket and came here is named Jeanie, and she's my soulmate."

The alphas' brows all rose, and the effect would have been comical if the issue at hand hadn't been so serious.

Alistair was the first to break into a smile. "Congratulations, Joss, that's wonderful. Fate is a damn funny thing, isn't it?"

Joss relaxed with a smile. "Indeed."

Atticus, Marcus, and Caesar each congratulated him on finding his soulmate.

Joss glanced at Brent, noticing that the male looked stoic and almost angry. But the male wouldn't look at him, keeping his head down and his arms crossed over his chest. Making a mental note to speak to the male after the meeting, Joss turned his attention back to the alphas.

"Now," Joss said, "I wanted to let you all know my good news, and to let you know what I was thinking about in terms of bringing Jeanie into this world."

"What did you have in mind?" Caesar asked.

"I want to bring her to the park after the tours are finished and take her to the maintenance shed in our paddock. There, I'll explain about our people and shift for her. My intention is to have a tent set up for us to spend the night together in the paddock, and then assuming all goes well, I'll bring my pack up Sunday morning to introduce her."

Marcus cleared his throat. "You know if you show her your shift that she won't be allowed to leave. If she freaks out, we'll have to keep her locked up somewhere."

Joss nodded. The thought occurred to him several times over the last week as he'd thought about the best way to bring her into his world. She was going to learn that there weren't only humans living on earth. That shifters, who were currently thought of as fairy tales, were actually real.

"I believe she'll be okay with it. I spoke to Devlin, and the human female soulmates, and every one of them said they felt a connection to their shifter mate that they couldn't really explain. Once they learned the truth of shifters, it all clicked into place, and they understood the need for secrecy. I wouldn't do anything to endanger our people."

"We know," Atticus said. "It actually makes sense now that I know you've found your soulmate. You've been acting quite different this last week. Downright happy."

Joss snorted. "I am. For the first time in I don't know how long."

"We always knew that it was a possibility that an alpha's soulmate might be found among the humans on the VIP tours, so it's not surprising, really, that after a year, one of us has finally found our other half," Caesar said. "I'm happy for you. I think the question is whether your pack will be okay with a human alpha female."

"It shouldn't matter," Marcus said. "An alpha's soulmate is no different than anyone else's soulmate."

"That's not entirely true," Joss said. "Caesar's not wrong. It's crossed my mind that while the pack may be fine with human soulmates for their members, having a human alpha female is an entirely different thing. The truth is that I don't know. There's nothing in our pack laws that state a human can't become a soulmate for a member, and membership in the pack is up to the alpha." Joss stopped speaking and looked at Brent, who was still not making eye contact with him. "It's why I want to share my shifting nature with her, then mate and mark her before I introduce her to the pack. Once she's mine in truth, no one can say anything against her. She'll be alpha female, period."

"You might have some push-back," Atticus said. "But I think it's smart to have her mated and marked first. Then there's no denying what she is to you. Assuming, of course, that she doesn't flip out at discovering the truth of shifters and try to run away."

Joss certainly hoped that she wouldn't. And he didn't think she would. She was smart and curious, and even though they hadn't spent a ton of time together in person, he felt like he'd known her for a long time.

"You're going to have some people with you when you do this?" Caesar asked.

Joss nodded. "I was thinking about Jenni and Devlin, and Auden and Jess."

Auden was one of his pack members and mated to an owl shifter. He hadn't told any of his pack members about Jeanie, but he knew he could trust Auden.

"I'll make sure Jenni and Devlin are available," Caesar said.

"Thanks."

Each alpha and his second-in-command wished him luck before leaving the room. When it was just Joss and Brent, the young male finally looked at Joss.

"You have something to say," Joss said. A statement, not a question.

"You're going to have a problem if you choose to mate a human."

"Our entire VIP tour program is based on our people finding their soulmates in humans, so why would you believe that anyone would care?"

"Because you're the most powerful male in the pack." Brent moved to the table, planting his hands on the top of one of the leather chairs. His knuckles cracked as he squeezed the material. "Your mate is powerful through you. She would wield the power of the alpha position."

"I know that."

"She knows nothing about us. How could she possibly be the alpha female? How could you be okay with bringing a weak human into our midst and giving her the authority to rule over our lives?"

Joss let out a growl and rose slowly to his feet, his wolf out and furious at the male's insolent tone. "I think you're the one with the problem."

Brent leaned back a little, his eyes flashing amber. "Humans can't be alphas. Period."

"She's my soulmate."

"Then step down."

"Not until I'm good and ready."

"You're inviting problems into the pack by mating a human. Who the hell cares if a random pack member finds his or her soulmate, but the alpha? Hell no. I won't come against you, but if someone calls you out in a battle, I'm not going to step between you either."

"Let anyone come against me, and I'll swiftly remind them why I'm alpha. I didn't get the position because I'm nice, I won it by blood." He moved so fast he startled Brent, slamming him against the wall by his throat. "I'm better than you. Bigger than you. Older and wiser. You will stand with me as my second, or I'll remove you from the position."

Brent bared fangs at Joss. He squeezed his throat a little tighter, restricting the airflow.

With an unhappy grunt, Brent tilted his head as much as he could and cast his gaze down to the floor in submission. Joss released his grip and folded his arms. "You're not some young pup who doesn't know any better. I'm the alpha. I'm the law. If you don't like it, you can leave, but neither you nor anyone else will stop me from making Jeanie my mate in truth."

Brent rubbed his throat. "I'm being realistic. Tell me if your human could take the life of someone she loved in the name of keeping our people safe. The way that you took Jesse's."

"I wouldn't put her in that position."

"If there was no choice, would she stand by you while you snuffed out the life of someone she cared about? Humans don't think about things the way we do. She couldn't possibly understand, and that will be your downfall. I'll stand by you because you're right—you're the law. But you're asking for a coup, and I'm not interested in dying because you've got a hard-on for a human."

Before Joss could answer, the young male was out the door, leaving him staring into the empty hallway.

Joss was pissed, but just like the alphas had suggested, it was possible that some of his people might balk at a human soulmate because he was alpha. In the end it didn't matter. He was going to mate Jeanie and bring her into his life. He'd teach her everything about shifters, and he'd be damned if he'd ever put her in a position where she'd have to make a life or death choice like he did.

He left the conference room and walked to the finance offices to speak to Devlin, texting Auden along the way to let him know he'd be coming to speak to him and his mate shortly. He looked at his screen. He needed to pick Jeanie up in three hours, which meant he didn't have much time to get everything ready.

Tonight, he'd show Jeanie who he really was.

He just hoped to hell she didn't freak out.

CHAPTER SEVEN

Jeanie looked out the window of the SUV as Joss pulled down an access road at one side of the park. The sun was setting, the dark night sky descending as the sun disappeared. He said he had a special night planned for them, and she'd dressed casually in her favorite pair of jeans and a short-sleeved shirt. As they neared a guard booth, a man inside waved them through.

"So are you going to tell me what we're doing here yet? You've been so quiet."

"Sorry," he said, pulling into a parking spot between several other identical SUVs. "I have something to share with you, but I want to get where we're going first and then tell you."

"Okay. I like surprises."

"Good."

He turned off the engine and they got out. He met her at the back of the SUV and took her hand. "Did I tell you how lovely you look?"

"You might have mentioned it a time or two," she said with a smile.

They walked to a gate and he used a code to unlock it. It opened slowly, creaking loudly. Two men approached wearing park uniforms.

"Are we all clear?" Joss asked.

"Yes, sir," one said. They both nodded at Joss and continued past them.

She and Joss walked on a dirt path to a locked gate, where he entered a code to open it. "Oh! This is the safari tour path."

"Yep," he said. The path was lit by low lights. "This is the service path."

"What are we doing on it?"

"We're... going on a picnic."

"Um, okay?" She laughed as he took her hand once the gate was locked behind them.

"Trust me."

"I do."

He looked at her quietly. "I cherish that, Jeanie. Truly."

She smiled up at him. He bent and kissed her.

As they walked along the path, she said, "It's pretty deserted."

"The tour closes at eight. The park is still open until ten, but there won't be any patrons around us."

She recognized the different paddocks along the tour, but aside from the one that contained deer, antelope, giraffe, rhinos, and the moose named Tank, they all appeared empty.

"Where are all the animals?"

"Away for the night."

She was going to ask what he meant by that, when they stopped in front of the paddock that held the wolves and he crouched down. He moved a decorative shrub to the side to expose a keypad. A lock clicked, and the fence made a shuddering sound. He put the shrub back into place and pushed the fence section, a gate appearing in the center.

"Whoa, are you nuts?" she asked as he stepped through the gate and held out his hand.

"You just said you trusted me. I swear on my life you won't get hurt. The wolves are all gone."

"How? You just said the animals were away for the night, but where did they all go?"

"Let's just say that they're not outside anymore, so we have the whole paddock to ourselves. And we'll also say that I'll explain everything in a minute."

She tentatively stepped through the gate. She couldn't see much in the paddock because the sun had set. She could see some darker shadows against the night sky, but she didn't see any glowing eyes or hear any angry growling.

"You're holding onto a lot of secrets right now."

"Yeah, sorry. I promise it'll all be worth it."

He put his phone to his ear and spoke a few words in a low tone, and in the distance, lights turned on. She could make out a low building and another smaller structure nearby. They walked toward the buildings, and as they drew closer she recognized the maintenance shed he'd told her about on the tour, and what looked like a table with two chairs, and a tent.

On the table were flickering candles, and two place settings.

They stopped in front of the maintenance shed, and he turned to face her. "You were right that I've got secrets, and it wasn't just me wanting to keep the location of our date tonight as a surprise." He sucked in a breath and let out a low grunt.

It looked like he was struggling with something. She took one hand from his and placed it on his cheek. "Whatever it is, just tell me."

He kissed her palm.

"I like you," he said.

"I like you, too."

"I want to tell you everything about me. And I want to start by saying that I don't just work here at the park. I live here, too."

"You do?"

He nodded. "I live here, because it's not really safe for me, or my people, to be outside in the world around humans."

He didn't say anything for a moment, just stared intensely down at her. She blinked a few times and frowned, the word 'humans' sticking out.

"What do you mean by humans? Are you an alien or something?" She tried to laugh off her question, but there was something really odd about the way he was looking at her. His eyes were suddenly amber and almost glowing.

"I'm not an alien." He gave her hand a squeeze and brought it to his lips. "I'm a shifter. I can become a wolf at will."

She started to laugh, but it died in her throat. "You're serious."

"Very much. I want to show you, but I want to make sure that you know two things."

She eyed him skeptically. "Okay."

"First, what I am, what my people are, can't ever be told to anyone else. And second, the reason I'm telling you this—when it's such a serious secret—is because I believe you're my soulmate. The one female on the planet meant for me."

Her mind spun. "People can't turn into animals, okay? I mean, I like you. Really, I do. But are you serious? If this is a joke, it's not even a little bit funny." She let go of his hand and crossed her arms across her chest.

"It's not a joke. I promise you that I'm serious. Not only with what I can change into, but how much the secret must stay here in the park. I need to know before I show you that I can trust you not to freak out."

"I'm not freaking out, I'm a little pissed to be honest."

"I'm sorry. I hated keeping this from you, but we have rules in place in these situations. It killed me to not be able to tell you everything that first night." He put his hand on the back of her neck and pulled her close. She caught the scent of his cologne, and immediately she thought about the woods.

And wolves.

"Please trust me," Joss whispered. "I'm trusting you with a secret that could destroy my pack if it got out."

The weight of his words settled on her. She closed her eyes when he pressed his forehead to hers. Tears stung her eyes, and she wasn't really sure why she was feeling emotional, except she'd finally heard the other word he'd used.

Soulmate.

"If I believe you," she said, swallowing against the lump in her throat. "If you're really what you say you are, does that explain why I want to be with you so much? Why I spent the whole week missing you like a phantom limb?"

He chuckled and kneaded her neck lightly. "Yes."

"I do trust you. And I'm glad you trust me."

He leaned away slightly and cupped her face. Giving her a kiss, he said, "I feel like you're not sure if you believe me."

"I... seeing is believing?"

"Indeed."

He pulled open one of the large doors on the shed and she blinked at the bright light emanating from inside. Two couples were standing there.

"Jeanie, this is Devlin and his soulmate Jenni, and Auden and his soulmate Jess. They're here to answer questions after I shift. I can't change back right away, but you won't have to wait too long. Then, if you're not freaked out, we can have dinner and talk."

She looked out the door, able to see more clearly with the light from the shed.

Her gaze landed on the tent. "What's the tent for?"

"I'm hoping you'll want to stay with me."

"You live in a tent?"

"What? No, I live underground in a private area with my pack. I can't take you there until we're officially mated. That doesn't have to happen tonight, but I want to stay with you. I want to wake up with you in my arms, Jeanie."

Her heart fluttered. "Okay."

He kissed her swiftly and took a step away, then unbuttoned his shirt. The dark material was tossed aside quickly, and she sucked in a breath, mesmerized by his sexy upper body. Stacked with muscles, he had the faintest dusting of hair across his chest. The tattoos she'd seen on his arm were fully visible now, the dark ink stretching in swirls and pictures from his shoulder to his wrist. Her gaze tracked his sexy abs, and she noticed his hands were resting on his unfastened jeans.

She lifted her head swiftly and blushed when she saw he was looking at her with an arched brow. "Like what you see, sweetheart?"

Her cheeks heated further, and she shrugged with a smile. "You know you're sexy."

"So are you."

He gave her a smile laced with heat. And then glanced beyond her to the two couples, clearing his throat noisily. She looked over her shoulder and saw that the two men turned their women away from Joss so they couldn't see him take off his clothes, and she smiled as she looked back to him. He continued to strip, revealing inch after inch of sexy skin. She'd never watched a guy strip the way he did, never taking his gaze from her as if she were the most important person in the world to him.

She wasn't sure if she really believed what he said about being able to become an animal. It was too fantastical. But he was so serious. And there was something about the whole situation that rang true to her, even though the rational part of her didn't think anything would happen. Except her getting to see him strip.

He toed off his shoes and shoved his jeans down his legs, revealing a thick, long cock that was fully at attention. He kicked his clothes aside and straightened, his hands loose at his sides, his eyes a bright amber.

"You ready?" he asked.

"You keep asking me that." It took a considerable amount of effort for her to lift her gaze from his pelvis, but she managed finally.

"Because you're distracted by my dick and I don't want you to freak out."

"I won't, I promise."

"I'll change forms and then you can ask the others questions if you want. In a little while I'll change back, and we can talk."

"I'm ready."

I think.

But ready for what, really? Was he really going to become a wolf? What would she do if he didn't?

What would she do if he did?

CHAPTER EIGHT

J oss had never tried to shift while he was turned on, but stripping for Jeanie while she watched his every move had made his body come to life. She thought he was sexy, but he'd never been attracted to a female like he was to her. His mouth watered at the thought of seeing her laid bare for him, tracing her sexy curves with his fingers and tongue. Hearing her call out his name.

He wanted all of it.

With her.

With the two couples turned away, Jeanie was the only one looking at him. He could see that she was skeptical, but that she hadn't just thrown up her hands and tried to leave spoke to her feelings toward him.

He inhaled and tried to settle his wolf, who wanted to carry her to the tent and make her theirs.

Reaching into himself, he kept his gaze on her and called for his wolf. The change was swift—from hands and feet to paws, from bare skin to fur. He shook himself out and sat down on his haunches, looking at Jeanie.

Her eyes were so wide it was almost comical. He sniffed

the air, finding the tangy scent of her fear which sat at the back of his throat and made his hackles rise. He didn't want her to be afraid, but he couldn't tell her that in his shift.

He let out a short bark, and Auden and Jess turned around.

"Jeanie? You okay?" Jess asked. She stepped up next to her and so did Jenni, the two females putting their hands on her in comfort.

"He's still Joss in there," Jenni said. "He's not a natural wolf. While he's got wolf instincts, he's still a man."

Jeanie's chest was rising and falling swiftly as she panted for breath, her brows furrowing as she stared at him. "It's not possible. I didn't just see that."

She closed her eyes and bit her bottom lip.

"It's real. Shifters are real," Jess said. "Joss is the alpha of the wolf pack, the most powerful male."

Jeanie opened her eyes. "The soulmate thing?"

"It's part of who shifters are," Jenni said. "Shifters have soulmates, and they know them on sight. It's like a key fitting into a lock. It just... makes sense."

Devlin nodded. "I'm human, Jeanie. When I met Jenni, I just knew that she was meant to be mine. I couldn't explain it, because there's this part of us being human that feels like relationships shouldn't move so fast. That we don't go from 'hello' to 'let's get married' in two seconds. You said you couldn't stop thinking about him all week. Did you want to come see him?"

"Every day," she said.

"I'm sure he'll tell you that he wanted to see you, too, but he didn't want to rush you," Auden said. He stepped out and looked between Joss and Jeanie. "Soulmates are precious. Trust me when I say that he wouldn't be sharing his shifting nature with you if you weren't meant to be his mate. Our people take the secrecy of shift extremely seriously."

"Do you understand?" Jenni asked.

Jeanie glanced at the lioness. "You're a wolf?"

"I'm a lioness," she said, smiling.

"I'm an owl," Jess said.

"I'm a wolf," Auden said.

"I understand the need for secrecy." Jeanie rubbed the space between her eyes with her thumb. "What now?"

"Do you have any questions we can answer?" Jess asked.

"Why don't you want humans to know about shifters?"

"Because it's too dangerous. Humans tend to kill first when they don't understand or are scared by something new."

"You've been around for a long time?"

"No one knows how long exactly," Jenni said, "but some of our people can trace their lineage back many generations. We think shifters have been around as long as humans, and probably lived among them at one time. Something happened between them that sent the shifters into hiding, though. It's why we're fairytales and not believed to be real."

"You can pet him," Jess said softly. "He's your soulmate. Touching him will make it real for you."

Joss straightened, his fur bristling in anticipation as Jeanie stared at him. She slowly closed the distance between them and touched one ear. She jerked her hand away and then giggled nervously. She laid her hand on the top of his head and he closed his eyes, enjoying her tentative touch. She dropped to her knees and ran her hand down his back, which made him want to arch like a cat and then roll over with his belly in the air.

He let out an appreciative, humming growl. He inhaled, finding her smelling less of fear and more of curiosity, the unpleasant bitter tang giving way to her naturally sweet scent. He leaned into her and she put her arm around him and settled her face on his shoulder.

"This still doesn't feel real," she whispered.

"Is there anything else we can answer for you?" Auden asked.

Jeanie turned her head to look at the small group. "I don't think so. I don't understand everything, but I do understand how serious this is and I promise the secret is safe with me. I'd never jeopardize Joss's safety, or anyone else's here."

"Then we'll leave you two alone," Jenni said.

The four said goodbye, opening the hidden door in the floor of the shed that lead down to the underground space. When the door closed behind them, Joss nuzzled Jeanie, and she leaned away a little and cupped his head.

"You're a good-looking wolf, Joss. If I hadn't seen it with my own eyes, I'd definitely think you were playing tricks on me. Do you want to walk around outside until you can change back?"

He nodded and she rose to her feet, and they headed outside and walked around the paddock. For a little while she was quiet, and then she started to talk.

"It's the craziest thing. Never in my wildest dreams would I have thought this was something that could actually happen. But here we are. You've got an animal inside you and so do other people here. I have a million questions but didn't want to hear it all from the others, I want to hear it from you." She sighed and stopped, looking up at the dark sky and the three-quarters moon partly covered with clouds. "Can you change back now? I have a question I do want to ask you personally and I want you to be able to answer me."

He let go of his shift and returned to his human form, energized by the adrenaline coursing through him and the wolfish tendencies that were still in the forefront of his mind. Pushing aside those animalistic thoughts, he said, "Ask away."

"Can I leave?"

His wolf howled in his mind.

"What do you mean?" he asked cautiously, not wanting to rush to judgment.

"I mean, are you going to ask me to just disappear? Like never go back to my house or job? I want to be with you. I mean, I feel like you're going to ask me to stay with you permanently. But I don't want anyone to worry about me. If I just... never showed up again, my friends would worry."

He let out a calming breath and smiled at her. "I do want you to move here to the park with me, and I don't want you to keep working at the diner. You don't have to give up your friends. We'll come up with a cover story for you involving a job and living arrangements here." He moved closer until their bodies were almost touching. "Will you be my mate, Jeanie?"

She gazed up at him, a multitude of emotions flickering in her eyes. She'd told him during one of their video calls that she hadn't been looking for a long-term relationship. She'd told her friend Regina that she was content to wait for Mr. Right. Joss hadn't really known what that meant, but Devlin had explained human females often believed their one-right-man was known generically as Mr. Right. Jeanie had confessed that night, a few days after their meeting, that she thought he was her Mr. Right, but she was scared about how fast things were moving.

When she didn't answer his question, he asked, "Are you still scared?" He cupped her face, and she sighed softly and tilted her head a little.

"Not really. I didn't understand why I was so drawn to you. That you're not really human actually makes sense, and in a way it makes me feel safer about how fast I felt things were moving for us. My feelings are so strong, I mean... can I be brutally honest?"

"Of course."

"I'm half in love with you. I can feel some kind of weird connection to you in my heart that I just can't explain."

Joss's wolf was elated, his heart soaring at her words. Even though she wasn't a shifter, she still recognized something special between them. "I don't want you to ever be scared of your feelings for me. I'm not like your ex. I'll never cheat on you. You're it for me for the rest of my life."

"I know you're not like him," she rasped, emotion rising in her voice. "You're not like anyone I've ever known. I want to be your mate, Joss. I want to stay with you. You're it for me, too."

He lowered his head and kissed her, his wolf rumbling out a contented, happy growl in his chest. He drew her against him with an arm around her back, his still-hard cock trapped between them.

She set trembling hands on his shoulders and then wrapped her arms around him. Deepening the kiss, he stroked his tongue against hers, fanning the flames of desire that engulfed him.

He eased from the kiss, smiling at her soft moan of disappointment.

Lifting her into his arms, he walked toward their date setup. "Are you hungry?" he asked.

"For you. We can eat later."

"Whatever you want, sweetheart."

"I just want you."

"You've got me, I promise."

He ducked his head and pushed through the tent flaps, putting Jeanie on the mattress on the tent floor. He reached up and found the end of the wire, switching on the tiny string lights he'd hung from the ceiling, softly illuminating the interior. Jeanie gasped as she looked around.

"It's like a bedroom in here!"

"I wanted you to be comfortable."

He'd searched online for ways to make the tent more romantic and cozy. He'd laid a thick rug on the floor and brought up a full-sized mattress, which he'd covered with a satin fitted sheet and topped with pillows. A small table held electric candles, which he switched on using a small remote. Finally, he turned on a small electric fire pit, which had a noiseless fan blowing air through fabric colored like flames, flickering lights adding to the illusion.

"This is really amazing, Joss," she said. "You did this for me?"

"Of course. I'd do anything for you, Jeanie."

"Where have you been all my life?"

"Not nearly close enough."

She took off her sandals and set them aside, then smiled at him. "I want to be yours, Joss."

"You already are."

"No, I mean officially. You said I couldn't be with you in the park until we're officially mated. I want that now, if you do."

He inhaled sharply, his fangs tingling in his gums. Dropping to his knees in front of her, he said, "I have to bite you while we make love."

"Where?" Her eyes went wide again.

He lifted his hand and placed it on her neck, stroking his thumb along the side. "Here. My fangs will come out and I'll bite you. It will hurt some, but I promise I'll do my best to distract you with pleasure. There's just one thing."

"What?" She whispered the word.

"When we do this, it'll be like we're married for me and my wolf, and for my people too. That means that not only will I need you to move into the park immediately with me, but you'll also be the alpha female of the pack. You'll be a leader."

Her brow furrowed. "That sounds ominous."

"It's not a bad thing, but there's never been a human alpha female of the pack. It's not against our laws, but it could be met with some opposition. You wouldn't be in any danger, but I might have to defend my position as alpha."

"Like fighting?"

He nodded.

"You don't seem worried."

"I'm alpha for a reason, and it's not because I'm charming."

She smiled. "You're very charming."

"I promise you're the only one who thinks that."

"Will your people hate me?"

"I don't think so. More that there might be those among them who don't want a human leading, even though I carry the power and you're only a leader through mating. I will stand against anyone who tries to come at me for mating with you, but even if I had to step down as alpha, sweetheart, I still would. You're my soulmate, and I could no more walk away from you than I could pull the moon from the sky."

"You'll teach me everything there is to know about shifters, right?"

"Absolutely. But later, of course. We have some things to attend to."

Her eyes darkened and she bit her lower lip. "We do?"

With a growl, he pushed her legs apart and leaned into her. Their lips met and he followed her down to the mattress.

The only thought on his mind: mine.

CHAPTER NINE

Jeanie was positively on fire. She'd honestly never wanted anyone as much as she wanted Joss. Her mind was still spinning from all that she'd learned. People changing into animals was the most fantastical thing she'd ever heard of, but seeing him turn into a wolf made sense in a strange way. Some part of her must have known they were meant to be together. She just wished she'd met him years ago.

He kissed across her cheek and tugged lightly on her earlobe, sending a riot of shivers down her spine. Then he kissed and sucked his way down her neck, tugging the collar of her shirt aside to place a few kisses on her collarbone. He levered himself up and smiled at her. He moved from between her legs and made swift work of her clothes.

She was really glad she'd shaved her legs.

He placed his warm hands on her knees, and slowly pushed them apart. She was reclined on her elbows, watching his face as his gaze dropped to the apex of her thighs. He spread her wide open. She'd never been laid bare like this before, but the vulnerable feeling only heightened her excitement.

Curling his hands over her upper thighs, he met her gaze for a long moment, and then lowered his head. The first stroke of his tongue up her folds sent her sprawling back on the mattress as heat washed over her.

He gripped her thighs tightly as he began to play with her, his tongue swirling around her clit and delving inside her. He snarled softly, tilting his head and tonguing her. She writhed under his attentions, moaning his name as he flicked his tongue rapidly over her clit, and pleasure washed over her as she came. He growled against her sensitive clit and she shuddered, reaching for him as her back arched.

In a heartbeat she found herself flipped to her stomach and hauled up onto her knees. She let out a gusty groan and looked over her shoulder as he rose up behind her and grasped his cock, pressing it against her heat.

He pushed into her, stretching her in the most delicious of ways. She threw her head back with a moan as he thrust hard, burying himself entirely within her. He didn't move for a long moment, squeezing her hips as he gave her time to adjust to him.

And then he was moving. Withdrawing and thrusting, setting up a fast rhythm that made her body light up again. He ran his hand up her back and leaned over, pressing her hips down and giving a snarling nip to her shoulder. She gasped at the contact and the deep way he penetrated her, loving how he seemed to know just how to move to take her higher.

Lowering her upper body to the mattress, she turned her head to the side and grasped the sheet under her. He growled and it sounded like he approved. He tilted her hips a little more and as he plowed forward, she gasped, the position sending shock waves all over her with each thrust.

"Mine," he said, leaning over her again and cupping her chin. He spanned his fingers on her throat as he quickened his pace, hitting the place inside her that made her whole body quake.

"Fuck," she moaned, closing her eyes as her pleasure built. Her hands clenched and her toes curled as he slammed into her over and over.

She was crying out his name as she fell over the edge into white hot bliss, the center of her body going molten, her pussy gripping his cock.

He followed her, his cock thickening and spasming within her. There was a deep snarl and then a pinch of pain as he bit her neck, fangs digging into her flesh. Her vision blurred as pleasure continued to flow within her, a connection to Joss snapping into place. It felt like love, but deeper and sweeter.

He extracted his fangs, and she caught the scent of blood a moment before he licked across the wounds. He slipped his hands under her and took her fully to the mattress. As he pulled from her body, she groaned at the loss.

She rolled to face him and kissed him.

"It's never been like that for me before," she murmured. "I feel so connected to you."

"Because we're soulmates. It's never been like this for me, either. You're mine, Jeanie. And I'm yours."

She kissed him again and settled her head on the pillow, stroking her fingers through his beard. "Do shifters get married?"

"If they want. A mating bond is stronger than a piece of paper, but I'd love if you had my last name."

She smiled. "I'd like that, too."

They kissed and talked some more in that lazy way that lovers did when it felt like they had all the time in the world. They made love a second time, slower but no less passionate.

He didn't stop until he'd wrung every ounce of pleasure from her. She'd never had so much pleasure in one night, his talented hands and fingers driving her wild.

Instead of eating at the table, Joss brought the prepared meals into the tent and they ate steak and baked potatoes, topping off the meal with chocolate layer cake and fresh fruit.

As she drifted off to sleep in his arms in the dark tent with the sounds of nature surrounding them, he promised to tell her everything about himself and his people in the morning.

"Goodnight, Alpha," she whispered, giving him one last kiss.

"Goodnight, sweet Alpha."

CHAPTER TEN

Joss hadn't known the sort of happiness that waking up next to Jeanie gave him. It was the kind of sweet feeling that filled his whole being. And his wolf was the most freaking content creature on the planet, practically purring as they lay twined up together with their soulmate.

He knew he needed to move on with the morning. He had a shit-ton of stuff to explain to Jeanie.

And he had to plan a pack meeting.

Jeanie stirred next to him, and he kissed her neck, right at the place he'd marked her.

"Morning," he murmured.

She said good morning couched with a yawn and rolled to her back.

"Feel different?" he asked.

"Because we're basically married?"

"Yeah. And you're alpha female of a pack of wolf shifters you didn't even know existed until last night."

"I feel different because I'm happy. I feel like you and I were meant to be together, and I never figured myself for being one of those girls who believes in soulmates, but here we are."

"Here we are." He kissed her and sat up, rolling his neck.

"And as unromantic as this statement is going to be, I have to pee. And there's no bathroom in this tent."

"No there isn't, but we can stop in the employee cafeteria. Let's get dressed."

They dressed quickly, then he grabbed his cell from his pocket, texting for some of the younger pack members to come and clean up the paddock in preparation for the tours later that afternoon.

Following the path away from the paddocks, he unlocked the employee cafeteria and chuckled as Jeanie made a beeline for the ladies' room as soon as she spied it.

He used the facilities and met her in the kitchen area, where he brewed them two mugs of coffee. They chose plates underneath heat lamps prepared by the bear shifters who handled the food, underground and topside. He was happy to find steak and eggs, and Jeanie chose a ham and cheese omelet.

They took a table near the window that looked out into the park. "It's one-way glass," he said. "We can see out, but no one can see in. Our people eat here on breaks, and there's also a market underground where we live that serves three meals a day."

"Plus all the fun park food?"

"Absolutely. I'm partial to the burgers."

"You're clearly a red meat kind of guy."

"Cause of my wolf, I suspect."

She hummed with a smile. "I'm supposed to work the dinner shift tonight."

His wolf snarled in his mind. But before he could say anything, she said, "But I'm going to tell them I can't work tonight and that I'm giving my notice."

He thought about her being away from the zoo for two weeks and his wolf didn't particularly like that.

Instead of saying what was on his mind, he said, "After we eat, I'll drive you to your place."

"Good, then we can go to the diner and I can tell Ron that I've got a much better offer."

Joss smiled. "Do you?"

"Sure. Well, not a job offer, but a really nice way to spend the rest of my life. When can I see your place?"

He dug his fork into a piece of rare steak and said, "I have to introduce you to the pack first. What happened between us is kind of unusual, so I need to handle it properly." He needed to get to the pack law books, which were down in his house. When he'd mated as a young male, she was a wolf. He'd gone to a gathering of packs to look for a mate and had found her. He brought her back and mated her in front of the pack, back in the days when wolf couples would bite each other in marking in public and then head to their home for the night to complete the mating.

Now, Joss had marked and mated Jeanie in private, but he still needed to mate her officially in front of the pack. It would be a symbolic marking, just a love bite on her neck, but it would mean volumes to the pack.

Jeanie tapped her fork on his plate. He blinked his eyes back into focus and looked at her. "Sorry, did you say something?"

"Yeah," she said with a smile. "I was asking what you're thinking about so seriously."

"The pack."

"Because of me?"

Nodding, he explained the marking ceremony. "But first, I need to bring you to the pack and introduce you. I think the sooner the better. There are already rumors swirling around the pack about me choosing a mate and it would be best to just get this part over with. Then we can schedule the mating ceremony for Monday or Tuesday night."

"Do I need to be nervous about tonight?"

"No. If anyone has a problem with me mating a human, I'll hear about it ahead of time. I'm going to gather my top-ranked males and elders and share the news. They'll ensure the pack knows what's going on before the meeting, so that it's not a surprise. If there are issues, I'll know going in."

"I hope your people like me."

"If any of them don't, you can't take it personally. It's not about you as a person."

"Yeah, it's about me as a human, which is something I can't control."

"Unfortunately, yes. Judging by how my second acted when I told him about you, I believe there may be a few who will protest. But would any of them challenge me for alpha? I don't really think so."

And he didn't. But he also wasn't a fool. If he didn't anticipate a challenge then he wouldn't be able to call himself much of an alpha. There were pack members who were pretty stuck in their ways. Like Brent, they didn't mind soulmates for the average wolf, but a human as alpha female? He had no idea how that was going to go down with everyone. But expecting the worst and hoping for the best seemed a good way to go about things.

They finished eating, and Joss took her home. Even though it rebelled with his wolf's nature to leave her, especially now that they were mated, he knew he couldn't just hang out with her all day away from the park when there were things to be handled. He needed to head off as many issues as he could, and that started with a meeting.

Joss walked up the stairs to the maintenance shed and out into the paddock. His ten highest-ranked males and the elders were milling about near the shed. They all looked curious, but it was clear that all of them knew something serious was going on. Joss shut the door to the shed and cleared his throat.

"Some of you may already know this, but a week ago I found my soulmate."

There were low, curious murmurs from the males, but no one spoke up.

"I found her on the VIP tour. And yes, that means she's human."

The murmurs grew louder, and Joss grimaced, letting out a low growl. The group quieted.

"You've mated with a human?" Vance, an elder, asked. "Without discussing it with the pack first?"

Joss folded his arms and let his wolf out a little. "I wasn't aware I needed to run anything by the pack first."

"Well, of course not, Alpha," Vance stammered, "but there's never been a human alpha female before. This is... unprecedented."

"Yes, it is. But I've read the laws, and there's nothing in them that says a human female can't be the mate of the alpha and take on the mantel of leadership alongside her mate."

There was an uncomfortable silence. Joss could feel the unease in the males.

"Listen," he said. "A couple hundred years ago, our people were living in the wild and fighting with natural animals for food and shelter. A human alpha female wouldn't be able to defend pack members the way that a wolf one would be. Back then? A human soulmate for any pack member was unthinkable. But we're not living back then, we're living in modern times. Packs aren't battling for territory and resources, so the need for our people to be solely shifters is long gone. You might have a problem reconciling a human alpha female at first, but I promise you that Jeanie is a wonderful female, and she's eager to learn about our people and help in any way she can. She's ready to give up her life outside the park and be with me, with our people full time. You couldn't ask for more."

"There will be rebellion within the pack," Derek said.

"From you?" Joss asked, lowering his arms and straightening his shoulders.

Derek dropped his gaze to the ground. "No. But others. I'd already heard rumors you'd mated someone, and it clearly wasn't one of the unmated females in our pack, so that left a human. Some of our wolves aren't happy about it."

Joss let that roll around his head for a moment. There were several things he could do about the dissension in the pack, but he wasn't sure that the disgruntled feelings weren't coming from a place of people who didn't like things changing. When the alphas chose to consider humans as soulmates, there were pack members who rebelled against the idea and loudly voiced their concerns. As time went on, and they saw that humans could be brought into the park without causing complete upheaval, they changed their minds.

But this situation was different. Joss wasn't simply a pack member—he was the leader. Jeanie was going to be their leader as well. Not only was this an untried concept, but the question of whether she could handle the burden of being Alpha was clearly being discussed. She'd have to prove herself, and the only way to do that was with time.

He wasn't going to kick anyone out of the pack for being afraid of change, but he would give them the option to leave. What he wouldn't tolerate, however, was disrespect to his soulmate.

"I would no more give up Jeanie as my soulmate than I would part willingly with a limb. If pack members are nervous, they need to decide if they want to stick it out or leave. I won't allow anyone to harm my soulmate or cause her to be harmed by their behavior or attitude. Spread the word that the pack is meeting tonight at nine in our private area." He leveled a hard look at the males with him. He trusted them to have his back, but things were different now, weren't they? Joss's human soulmate was throwing a wrench into things, but they would make it work. In time, the whole pack would come to treasure her as he did.

He hoped.

CHAPTER ELEVEN

Jeanie waited for Joss to pick her up, ready with a bag he'd told her to pack for the night. She'd offered to drive to the park, but he'd nixed the idea. He'd called in the early afternoon and said he had some concerns over how the pack introduction would go, but that it didn't change anything about their situation. She was his soulmate, and that meant she was alpha female of the wolves, period.

The idea still sounded so strange to her. Alphas. Wolves. Packs.

But she trusted Joss, and if he said it would be fine, then it would be. He was the first alpha to find his soulmate, although he'd explained that the bear alpha Marcus had a soulmate years earlier who'd died, and it was the general belief that shifters only got one soulmate in a lifetime.

It had been a hard day for her. It was strange, but being away from Joss for the day was difficult. She'd had trouble concentrating, her mind drifting to him constantly. He'd told her that once they were mated, he'd have trouble being away from her, but she was feeling the same difficulty. She'd gone into the diner planning to give Ron two weeks' notice as she'd discussed with Joss, but instead she told him that it was her last shift and she wouldn't be back. She explained she'd been given a great job opportunity at the safari park that included living arrangements. Her boss had asked her to reconsider, but he hadn't been able to make her change her mind. Even if she did feel a little guilty for leaving him in the lurch.

When Joss had texted to say he was on the way to pick her up, Jeanie knocked on Glennis's door, but she hadn't been home. She'd left a message for her explaining she was moving in with her new boyfriend and would be paying out the rest of her month's lease and moving out immediately. Once her bag was packed, she sat on the couch in the family room, waiting for Joss.

An odd feeling came over her. She could feel Joss coming near.

She opened the front door, smiling when she saw him getting out of an SUV.

He jogged up the sidewalk and lifted her off her feet, carrying her inside and kicking the door shut. Before she could say anything, they were kissing, and he was holding her tightly against him. A few breathless minutes later, he put her gently on the floor and smiled down at her.

"Hi."

She giggled. "Hi. I missed you."

"I definitely missed you."

She told him that she'd felt him close by before she'd known he'd arrived.

"Because we're soulmates," he said. "Even though you're human, our connection is strong enough that you can sense me. It's pretty damn cool."

"I thought so, too."

He picked up her bag and they left, heading to the park.

She leaned over and rested her head on his shoulder.

"Wow, you're tense. It's like leaning against a brick wall."

He rolled his neck. "Sorry, sweetheart. My wolf drove me nuts all day."

"Because we weren't together?"

"Yes."

"And?" She felt like it wasn't just that he'd missed her.

He rested his head against hers for a moment and sighed, then straightened. "When I spoke to the high ranked males and elders after I dropped you off earlier, they weren't as supportive as I expected."

"Because I'm human."

He grunted in agreement.

She chewed her bottom lip and looked out the windshield for a few moments, the scenery blurring by. "What does it mean, then?"

"I'm going to announce you tonight to the pack when we get to the park. We're mated and you're wearing my mark. Nothing anyone can do or say will change that, all right?"

She could feel him waiting for her response. Shifters were so different than humans.

"Okay. What will happen after the announcement?"

"I'll set up a date for our mating ceremony. It can be as soon as tomorrow night if you'd like."

She hummed and rubbed her cheek on his shoulder, hooking her arm through his and spreading her fingers on his forearm. "I mean what's really going to happen?"

"If someone has a problem with me taking you as my mate because you're human and they don't want a human alpha female, then they can challenge me for leadership of the pack."

"Challenge means fight, right?"

"Yes."

"Can you ignore the challenge?"

"No. The laws are pretty specific about when someone

can challenge an alpha and among them are when he chooses a mate or finds his soulmate. If someone's been wanting to challenge me and have been waiting for the right opportunity, now is the time."

She thought it was absurd that anyone in the pack would believe he wasn't a good alpha anymore simply because she was human. He was following his heart. Wasn't that what good leaders did?

"I find this super frustrating," she said.

He chuckled mirthlessly. "I know, sweetheart. It's not how I want things to go, but if it does, I'll deal with it."

"*We'll* deal with it," she reminded him.

He glanced at her and nodded, his eyes simmering with emotion. "I don't want you to be scared by anything anyone says or does. I'm alpha for a reason. If I have to fight, I will win. But even if something were to happen, if by some slim chance I were to lose the challenge, you and I would still be able to be together. They can take the alphaship away from me, but they can't separate us."

A little frisson of fear worked up her spine. Joss was anticipating a fight in her honor. He'd told her that he almost killed his brother because he wouldn't submit during their challenge. What if whoever challenged Joss didn't offer a way out? What if he wanted to kill Joss to take over?

Joss pulled over suddenly and pressed the button to activate the hazard lights. She sat up in surprise, her mouth open to ask him what was wrong. But then he turned to face her, his eyes glowing amber. "Don't be frightened."

"I'm not afraid of you."

"No," he said, shaking his head. "Don't be scared about meeting the pack. You won't be harmed. If I must battle tonight, I'll do it for you and for me. I was born to be alpha, but now that you're in my life, I would gladly walk away from everything for you."

"I don't want you to lose anything because of me." Emotion welled within her, her mouth going salty and her eyes stinging.

Joss cupped her face. "You're worth the world to me, Jeanie. I don't plan to lose the alphaship, but if I do, I'll still count myself the luckiest male on the planet for having found you. You're everything. Don't doubt that."

"This isn't like anything I've ever been a part of. I feel like a liability."

"You're not. You make me want to be a better male. The pack would be lucky to have you as an alpha female. You'll balance my rougher edges."

She laughed and tears trickled down her cheeks, which he gently wiped away. Giving her a kiss, he said, "Trust in me to keep us both safe, sweetheart."

"I will."

After another kiss, he pulled back onto the road and they continued their journey to the park. He parked the SUV and they entered through the employee gate, walking toward the employee cafeteria. She'd only been in the paddock and the cafeteria, but he'd explained the pack lived underground in a private area, as did the other shifter groups in the park. It amazed her that so many different groups of shifters lived and worked together, and humans were none the wiser. Aside from wolves, there were elephant, lion, bear, and gorilla shifters, plus three shifter mates who were unique— an owl, a black panther, and a red fox. There were five human soulmates—two for lions, two for gorillas, and one for a bear. She was thankful not to be the only human among all the shifters.

Joss entered a code at a door at the back of the cafeteria and they walked into a hall where he entered another code that opened into a stairwell leading down. At the bottom of those stairs was another security door and a code.

"You guys take security pretty seriously around here," she mused as he pulled the door open and let her walk by.

"We have to. It would be devastating to our people if humans found out about us."

"Are there other things out there besides shifters?" she asked.

"Things?" He arched his brow as he looked down at her.

"You know what I mean. I read a paranormal romance book once about a witch. So are there witches and other paranormal people out there?"

"There's a lot more out there than what we know about, for sure," he said. "There are people who have special abilities like telekinesis or who have magical powers. There are fairies out in the world as well, but like shifters, they stay away from humans and keep to their own kind."

"Do you think there are aliens?"

He snorted. "If there are, I've never met one."

"It would be pretty neat to meet a fairy. But I'm partial to wolves."

He growled softly and smiled at her again. His head snapped up and he stopped, putting his arm in front of Jeanie and taking a step to put himself in front of her. Ahead of them, blocking the long hallway, were two older men.

One of them put his hands up. "We're not here to cause trouble, Alpha. We were alerted you arrived and were waiting for you."

Joss relaxed fractionally, his arm dropping to his side. "Why are you waiting?"

"Because we wanted to meet your soulmate," the other said. He smiled at Jeanie. "I'm Vance, one of the pack elders."

The other man smiled at her as well, but there was something off about the way he smiled. It didn't reach his eyes. "I'm Amos, also an elder."

Joss said, "This is Jeanie Moon, my soulmate."

"It's nice to meet you."

Vance inclined his head. "For us as well. Joss has been alone for a long time. It's good for males to find their soulmates. Makes us feel whole."

"The pack's waiting for you," Amos said, reaching for the door.

Joss looked down at Jeanie and mouthed, "Are you ready?"

She nodded. Pushing the nerves away as much as she could, she plastered a smile on her face and took Joss's hand. Inside, she stifled a gasp as she looked around the huge room with walls and ceiling painted like the forest, and rock-covered homes that looked like dens. One of the homes was Joss's, where she'd be moving in with him tonight.

Joss had told her there were over fifty members of the pack, from the youngest at eighteen to the elders who were in their seventies. There were three unmated wolf ladies in the pack, and many of the men weren't mated. Everyone watched them in silence as they approached, the elders joining the pack and leaving Joss and Jeanie to stand alone.

Clearing his throat, Joss said, "I know most, if not all of you, have heard that I found my soulmate at the VIP tour. Her name is Jeanie Moon, and she's human."

There was a murmur throughout the pack, but Jeanie couldn't make out any words.

Joss lifted his hand and the pack quieted. "I've already mated and marked her, which makes her my alpha mate and your alpha female. I want you to welcome her to the pack and treat her as you would any other soulmate—with honor and respect."

Jeanie's cheeks were heating. She hadn't ever felt so many eyes on her before. Joss gave her hand a squeeze and she looked up at him, finding him smiling in encouragement at her.

"Hi everyone," she said, clearing her throat when her voice wavered slightly. "I look forward to getting to know you all."

A couple stepped forward, and the woman hugged Jeanie. "I'm so happy to meet you! Our alpha has been alone for far too long. It makes males grumbly when they don't have someone to love and support them."

"Hey!" the man said next to her.

Jeanie chuckled as the woman took a step back. "I'm Anke and this is my mate, Zeger. We work in the marketplace at a small shop. You can get anything you need from us—clothes, accessories, toiletries, even a cell phone. Just stop by anytime or call."

"It's nice to meet you," Jeanie said. "Thank you so much."

Once Anke and Zeger had broken the ice and came forward, the rest of the pack followed suit, and Jeanie was shaking hands and getting hugs from women, and being congratulated on mating the alpha.

"When will your mating ceremony be?" Jess asked as she came with Auden and gave Jeanie a hug.

"We were thinking tomorrow night," Jeanie said. Joss nodded in approval.

"Wonderful!" Anke said, clapping her hands. "Alpha, we'll handle everything. If you can manage to be without your lovely soulmate for an hour."

"An hour?" Jeanie asked.

A woman who identified herself as Auden's mother Delilah grinned. "The alpha has some special things to do ahead of the mating ceremony. It's tradition for the female to be with her family before the mating ceremony, but as you're human we'll happily stand in for you."

"Definitely," Jess said, smiling.

Jeanie fielded questions from several of the women as Joss spoke to the high-ranked men.

Jess leaned in and said softly, "Only the males are ranked in the pack. They start off as unranked males when they first shift and then they fight their way up through the ranks."

Jeanie smiled in thanks, her shoulders drooping in relief at the warm welcome. She caught Joss's gaze and smiled at him, and he nodded with a wink.

Nearly two hours later, after she'd met everyone in the pack and spent time with several of the ladies discussing the plans for the mating ceremony including what her favorite foods were, Joss picked up her bag and took her to one of the small homes. He opened the door but didn't let her cross through. He shouldered her bag and lifted her into his arms.

"I think this is the human way to enter a couple's home on their first night, yes?" he asked.

Her stomach flipped at his sweetly chivalrous move. "Definitely."

He carried her through the door, kicking it shut and stopping to drop her bag and twist the lock on the handle. He carried her into a bedroom, setting her gently on the bed and clicking on a small lamp on the nearby nightstand. He straightened and looked down at her, cupping her face with his large, warm hand.

"Sweetheart," he said, his voice low and growly. "I love you. Not because my wolf is crazy about you. Not because I believe you and I were destined to be together. But because you're amazing. You're sweet and honest, kind and funny. And so, so beautiful. We're already mates, but I want you to be my wife, too. I'll ask you properly and get you a ring, but I didn't want a moment to pass by without you knowing that I'm one hundred percent yours, all the way to the center of my being."

She let out a shaky breath, her heart fluttering. "I love you too, Joss."

CHAPTER TWELVE

Joss swung the ax, neatly severing the log into two
pieces. He picked up the smaller section and tossed it
toward the pile for the bonfire later that night, then
lifted the ax a second time, splitting the larger piece in two.
He set the ax down and tossed the pieces to the side, where
Auden and Alfie were setting them on the stack. It was tradition for the male to prepare the wood for the bonfire that
would be lit before the ceremony, because it was believed
that the longer the fire burned, the better the mating
would be.

Normally, the pack only celebrated matings on the full
moon, but because Joss was alpha and Jeanie was human,
he'd wanted to move the ceremony date up as soon as possible. He'd had concerns about delaying the ceremony for the
full moon, judging by how his high-ranked males and the
elders had acted when he'd told them about Jeanie. But then
the pack had really seemed to rally around them the night
before. Most seemed genuinely happy he'd found his soulmate, and although there were some who appeared to be

wary of having a human alpha female, everyone had been kind to her, and that's what he cared about.

He hadn't wanted to get into a battle last night, but he'd been prepared to defend his position and his mate. While he was thankful that he hadn't needed to shed blood in front of Jeanie, he couldn't help but feel as though something was off. A few of the males—particularly Brent and his father Vance—seemed disingenuous, as if their congratulations weren't honest. He hadn't shared the concern with Jeanie because he hadn't wanted her to worry. She had enough to do taking a crash course in pack law thanks to Anke and Delilah. The two females had been happy to help Jeanie learn about the mating ceremony and as much about pack life and the wolves as they could fit into the afternoon. The three females were sitting in the shade of the barn on a red gingham blanket and talking quietly, three of the law books spread out in front of them.

"She's really eager to learn," Auden said, brushing off his hands. "That's going a long way with the pack."

"I think so, too," Joss said. He looked at the young male. "Have you heard anything about her or the mating ceremony?"

Auden shook his head. "Nothing bad. My parents said it was about time you found your soulmate. I think you finding your soulmate through that VIP tour has helped our people feel a little better about the tours."

"What do you mean?"

"Well, no wolves have yet found a soulmate through the tours. Hell, only two humans who are soulmates have actually come through."

Alfie joined them. "To be honest, I've been feeling the same way. We put in hours of time and tons of work for the tours and only two soulmates have been found. It's... disheartening."

"I get it," Joss said. "I think all the alphas believed it would bring in more soulmates than it has. For sure I did. We did just send out another round of the coupons, though, so hopefully that will encourage more people to come into the park. I'd love for all our unmated males and females to find their soulmate."

"You and me both," Alfie said.

Joss finished cutting the wood and then set about digging the hole for the firepit and lining it with stones. By the time he was done, it was well past lunch and he was ready for a break.

Jeanie smiled at him as he sat down heavily on the blanket and wiped the sweat from his brow with his t-shirt. Anke and Delilah excused themselves, and Joss leaned over and kissed his mate. "You're so sexy," she murmured.

"Oh?" he asked with a chuckle.

She opened a cooler and handed him a bottle of chilled water. "It was hard to concentrate on the law books with you being all macho chopping wood, especially when you took off your shirt."

"Too bad we can't do something about it."

"Aren't you the alpha?" she asked, giving him a raised eyebrow.

"Of course, and so are you," he said. "But even alphas have to abide by rules."

"We can't go fool around because it's the day of our mating ceremony? I don't like that rule. Can I change it?"

He barked out a laugh. "That rule you can't change. At least not before you officially become the alpha female. It's not a bad rule. Waiting will make it better, don't you think?"

She made a face. "I'm not one for delaying satisfaction, Joss."

"It'll be worth it." His wolf was in agreement with her,

though. He wanted to take her somewhere private and see how many times he could make her shudder in bliss.

Looking skeptical for a moment, she dissolved into laughter and threw her arms around his neck. "I can't wait."

They ate a light meal of sandwiches and chips that Anke had packed for them in the cooler, and then they stretched out in the shade, his beauty resting her head on his chest, and talked. He couldn't believe how different his life was because of the VIP tours. He'd never have another lonely night because Jeanie was in his arms. He was the happiest damn wolf on the planet.

He wanted that for his people, too. He wanted the VIP tours to work their magic. He just didn't know how to make that happen.

Down in their home underground, Joss snarled at the closed bathroom door where Jeanie was getting ready for their hour-long separation. She'd showered. Without him! And was getting dressed. Without him!

He was wearing a pair of black trousers and nothing else, the traditional clothing for the male during the mating ceremony. Because Joss didn't have any family left—no males to stand with him during this time—he'd reached out to his closest friends and asked Trace and Randall to be with him. They'd happily agreed.

"I heard that," Jeanie said, opening the bathroom door and stepping out.

"Heard what?" he asked, feigning innocence.

"Your growl. You're the one who said we couldn't change the rule about no sex before the mating ceremony, not me. It's entirely your fault."

Out in the family room, he heard both males snicker and attempt to hide their delight with coughs.

He rose from the bed and grabbed her close. "I can't help it that I want you, sweetheart. You're the definition of temptation."

Her eyes were bright with happiness. "You are, too. Shut the door, they can wait," she whispered.

He growled her name softly, the sound more purr than anything. "Temptress."

She looked ravishing in a strapless black dress that fell to mid-thigh. She had black sandals on, and she'd pulled up the sides of her hair to reveal the mating mark on her neck. He lightly pressed his thumb to the mark. "In the old days, the couple waited until the ceremony to mark each other, which meant that they weren't hazed with pleasure when it happened."

"Yikes," she said. "I barely felt your fangs in my neck because you made me feel so good beforehand."

He smiled. "I'm glad for that."

"I wish I could bite you tonight, though." She wiggled her brows at him with a grin.

His whole body reacted to the idea, his skin tingling at the thought of her blunt teeth sinking into his skin. "You can."

"But I thought only the guys marked their ladies?"

"They do. But damn if my wolf wants you to bite me." He turned her swiftly, pulling her back against his chest and brushing her hair from her shoulder to bare her neck. He wrapped his arms around her, caging her to him. Then he lowered his head and spoke against her skin, sending a shudder through her. "You can bite my wrist while I bite your neck. Neither of us will break the skin, but it's symbolic. I'd love for you to give me a bruise that'll last for a while so I can enjoy your mark on my skin."

He lifted his hand slowly, and she kissed the inside of his wrist and then sighed breathlessly as she leaned against him. "I'm on fire, Joss. The things you do to me."

"Later, minx." He kissed her neck and released his hold on her. Reluctantly. "I can hear the females waiting for you."

"It's just an hour, right?" she asked as she turned and kissed him once.

"The longest hour ever."

"Love you. Big, bad wolf."

"I love you, sweetheart."

CHAPTER THIRTEEN

Outside of the house, Anke and Jess introduced Jeanie to three other wolf ladies—Desiree, Heidi, and Sarah.

"We've got an hour," Anke said. "We're going to have a snack at my place and chat, and then head up to the paddock when it's close to the time."

"Are you nervous?" Jess asked Jeanie.

"Yes and no. It's hard to explain."

"I get it," Jess said. "My people didn't do ceremonies like this, so it was strange to me. Even though I was already mated to Auden, I still had butterflies in my stomach."

Jeanie smiled. "That's pretty much how I feel."

Anke opened the front door and ushered everyone inside. The coffee table had been set with snacks and drinks, and they all sat and filled little plates with treats.

"Do you have any questions about the ceremony or wolves in general that we can answer?" Heidi asked, tucking a lock of dark hair behind her ear.

Jeanie finished chewing her bite of a mini cheese tart and said, "I spent the day reading about your laws and talking to

Anke, plus Joss has been so great to answer all my questions. Are you all mated?"

The three women wolf shifters each shook their head. "Not a whole lot of unmated males come through the VIP tours," Sarah said. "So we'll either stick it out and hope one shows up, or we'll choose a male and mate with him."

"Even though humans don't have a soulmate situation quite like shifters do," Jeanie said, "there are a lot of women out there who face the same choices—wait for Mr. Right or move on with Mr. Okay. I did."

Heidi's brows rose. "You were mated before?"

"Married, yes. He cheated on me with more than one woman and had a kid with one of them. I'm not sure why I stuck it out so long when I knew he wasn't a good guy, but I did. I divorced him a few years ago, and I'm so glad I did, so I could be available to be with Joss."

Everyone smiled at her words except Desiree. She looked as if she were trying to be happy but wasn't quite able to do it. Jeanie was about to ask her what was wrong when Anke said it was time for them to head up to the paddock.

They left Anke's home and headed toward the door that lead to the stairs up to the maintenance shed.

At the door, Desiree said, "Aw, shoot. I was supposed to bring the trays from the cafeteria up to the paddock."

"Why didn't you do that earlier?" Anke asked. She pulled open the door.

"I forgot. I can't carry them by myself." She looked right at Jeanie.

"I can help," Jeanie offered. It was hard not to feel obligated to assist with the intense way that Desiree was looking at her.

"Nah, you're not supposed to do anything but go up into the paddock to mate with Joss," Sarah said. "I'll go."

"You can both come," Desiree said. "It'll just take a few minutes, we'll be right up into the shed."

Before anyone could say anything else, Desiree grabbed Jeanie and Sarah by the hands and tugged them to another door that would lead up into the cafeteria. As they walked up the stairs and drew close to the door of the employee cafeteria, Jeanie's spine began to tingle in warning, the hairs on the back of her neck rising.

Jeanie stopped two steps from the top. "Something's wrong."

She glanced behind her at Sarah. "What?" the young woman asked.

Desiree turned slowly with a black plastic device in her hand. She moved so fast that she was a blur to Jeanie, punching the device into Sarah's stomach and clicking a button. Electricity crackled, and Sarah's body jolted hard, then she tumbled backward down the stairs. Jeanie let out a scream, but it was cut off midway when Desiree pointed the stun gun her way.

"Move, bitch."

"Wh-where?" Jeanie asked, a lump the size of a bowling ball in her throat. Sarah wasn't moving at the bottom of the stairs, blood seeping from a head wound.

"Up. Someone's been waiting to meet you."

Desiree opened the door to the cafeteria and pushed Jeanie through. She stumbled as her sandal caught on the tile and she fell, her arms flailing to catch herself. She managed to lean as she fell and bounced against the wall, stopping her downward tumble. Rubbing her bruised shoulder, she straightened, warily meeting Desiree's menacing glare.

Jeanie was kicking herself. She'd thought something was

off about the woman, but she'd traipsed right along with her to an obvious trap.

"What's this about? Why did you hurt Sarah and what the hell do you want with me?"

"I couldn't care less about that female. You, on the other hand, are a way for the rightful alpha to take his position."

"What are you talking about?"

Desiree shoved her forward, and they walked into the cafeteria. There were three men standing by the windows. The lights were off in the main room, but the kitchen was illuminated, and she could make out their features as they turned around. The one in the middle looked like a slightly older version of Joss, except for the gruesome scars that streaked his face.

"Sid?" Jeanie asked.

The moment his name left her lips, the man moved like a blur, back-handing Jeanie with enough force that she spun in a full circle and crashed to the ground. A foot connected with her stomach, making her scream in pain, the air whooshing from her lungs. She was wrenched to her knees by her hair and a fist connected with her eye, hair ripping out at the root as she was slammed backward into the tile.

She'd never so much as been slapped before in her life.

Now, she rolled to her side and spit blood out of her mouth, barely stifling a moan as pain rocketed through her.

"You don't ever say my name," Sid said. "I'm alpha."

The words of disagreement caught in her throat. She didn't want to be hit again. Worry for her safety went out the window as she realized that Sid must be at the park to fight Joss for the position of alpha. Joss had said one of the few times an alpha could be challenged was when he took a mate.

Jeanie pushed herself to a seated position, groaning internally at a wave of nausea. Wiping the blood from her chin, she said, "How did you know?"

Sid's brow rose. "Smart bitch, isn't she?"

The two males with him chuckled darkly.

Jeanie's heart kicked up a notch at the malevolence in their gazes.

"Desiree here," Sid said, as he tossed a length of rope to her, "couldn't leave with me because her mother was ailing. Instead, she spied for me, knowing that it would take Joss finding his soulmate to give me an in. All you need to know, however, is that at the end of this night, you're going to die."

Jeanie didn't want to cry. She didn't consider herself a particularly weepy person except for the sappy animal shelter commercials and tug-on-your-heart holiday movies. But she couldn't stop the hot tears that welled up in her eyes as Desiree bound her wrists tightly together and gagged her with a piece of fabric. She was jerked to her feet and had no choice but to follow as the small group left the employee cafeteria and headed toward the paddocks.

Her hopes of being rescued by the security patrol were dashed when she overheard the three men discuss the predictable patrol schedule, and how easy it was to gain access to the park after hours. She looked around, peering into the darkness for signs of life, but found none. It was only the five of them on the path that ran along the paddocks.

Joss had promised to keep her safe, but his words were a hollow comfort to her now. She'd become his doom. If it weren't for her, there wouldn't be a man stalking toward Joss with the intention of killing him. If it weren't for her, none of this would be happening.

Joss took a long-handled lighter from Eugene and lit the kindling in the firepit. It caught swiftly and blazed to life, the flames licking across the surface of the logs. Handing the lighter back to Eugene, Joss added another few armloads of wood to the fire. It needed to last through the ceremony and the party that followed, and he was certain that the massive amount of wood he'd cut and laid in the firepit would easily burn until dawn.

"Looks good, Alpha," Eugene said. He smiled at the fire and then at Joss.

"Thanks." He glanced at his watch and Eugene chuckled softly.

"This is so much better than how we used to do things," Eugene said.

Joss agreed. They used to make the couple stay apart for twelve hours before the ceremony. It was considered good luck if the male could stop himself from shifting and hunting down his female. His mind flitted to his former mate and their ceremony. While similar, everything felt new to Joss because Jeanie was his soulmate. He already felt far more connected to her than he'd ever felt to anyone before, and nothing made him happier than being with her.

For a moment, he wondered if he should've told her about his son, but he swiftly dismissed the thought. He'd tell her after they were fully mated and she was alpha female. She'd been reading in the pack's law and history books and was learning about the often-brutal nature of their people. He knew she would probably never fully understand what it was like to have a predator share her brain and body, but she was trying, and he loved her for it.

No, today was for happier thoughts and a wide-open future with Jeanie by his side and in his arms.

The maintenance shed doors opened and he saw three figures illuminated in the doorway. With a frown, he said, "Weren't there others with Jeanie?"

Eugene hummed. "I thought so. Anke, Jess, Jeanie..." He

ticked the names off on his fingers. "Desiree, Sarah, and Heidi. I wonder where everyone is?"

They watched as the three figures moved toward the bonfire, and the moment Joss realized that Jeanie wasn't among them, his wolf rose in his mind, fury and worry twining within him.

"Where's Jeanie?" Joss demanded.

"She's coming," Anke said. "Desiree needed help with some trays in the cafeteria and took Sarah and Jeanie with her. I'm sure they'll be right behind us."

Jess nodded. "We offered to go, but Jeanie volunteered."

"Trays? What trays?" Delilah asked, joining them.

"I don't know," Anke said. "She said she was supposed to bring trays from the cafeteria here."

Delilah shook her head. "No. Everything was already brought from the cafeteria, and besides, Desiree was never helping with the setup. That female always shirks her duties."

A chill went through Joss.

Where was Jeanie?

He scanned the paddock. The pack was milling around, some working at the tables where the meal would be served afterward, some speaking in small groups. Behind him three of the elders were waiting. Normally, Joss handled the mating ceremony as alpha, but since he was the one getting mated he'd asked Amos to perform it.

Joss felt a strange presence nearby, and somewhere in the darkness he heard a soft whimper. His heart clenched as fear washed over him. But it wasn't his own fear he was feeling, it was Jeanie's.

Turning slowly, Joss faced the elders and found two of them looking confused and one of them staring right at him.

"Amos," Joss said.

"I'm sorry it had to be this way," Amos said.

Stepping into the golden glow of the fire was Sidney, the

brother Joss had nearly killed all those years ago when he took over as alpha. Time had ravaged his features, the battle scars on his face looking even deeper.

Joss's fangs tingled in his gums. "What are you doing here, Sid? You were banished from the pack and this territory."

"Indeed," Sid said, tilting his head and giving Joss a maniacal smile. "But I have a ticket."

Bound at the wrist by rope and with a gag in her mouth, Jeanie was forced to her knees next to Sid, Desiree pointing a taser at her. Two other males were behind them, and Joss recognized them as his brother's friends, who'd willingly left the pack to follow Sid.

White-hot rage blasted through Joss as he saw Jeanie's bloodied nose and blackened eye, her cheeks streaked with tears.

Sid grasped a chunk of Jeanie's hair, making her whimper in pain, and gave a dark look to Joss. "Tonight we battle, brother. When you lose, you *both* die."

CHAPTER FOURTEEN

The pack was silent, watching the exchange between Joss and his brother. They were forbidden from interfering in an alpha challenge.

Joss let his gaze slide to Desiree, who was looking at Sid with complete adoration. "You've been spying for him the entire time." It wasn't a question, because Joss knew there was no way Sid would have been able to find out what was going on in the pack without someone on the inside. That it was Desiree was a surprise, but thinking back, he could remember the two used to fuck around.

Desiree gave him a dirty look. "I had no choice. Sid's the rightful alpha."

"I won the challenge," Joss said. "And I spared Sid's life."

"Pity," Sid said. "I won't be so generous with you."

"Let Jeanie go, and you and I will settle this once and for all."

Sid tapped a clawed fingertip against his chin. "Nah. She's going to be front and center to your downfall. If you beg me nicely, I might kill her swiftly before I send you into the afterlife. But if not, maybe I'll let my boys have her for a while."

Eugene took a step forward with Zeger and Auden. "This isn't the way our people handle alpha battles," Eugene said. "We don't harm innocents in the process."

Sid's gaze slid slowly to the three males who stood with Joss. "I'm alpha. I will do as I please, period."

"You're not alpha yet," Auden retorted.

"Pretty mouthy for a male mated to a puny bird," one of Sid's cronies said loudly.

"Hey!" Jess said from where she stood with Auden's mother behind them. "Fuck you!"

Joss looked at Jeanie. He could see something had changed in her demeanor. She didn't look frightened anymore, she looked pissed. Probably, she was pissed at him because he'd failed to keep her safe. It had never occurred to him that someone would go after her to get to him, let alone that it would be his brother who'd used a spy for two decades.

"I think," Sid said, tilting Jeanie's head and making her gasp through the gag, "that you probably didn't tell her all that you did as alpha. Maybe before you both die she should know."

"Shut your mouth," Joss said.

"I knew you hadn't told her," Sid said, chuckling. "Such a coward."

Jeanie gasped as he drew her up by her hair, her knees leaving the ground and her feet scrambling to get purchase in the dirt. "After he failed to protect his first mate from getting harmed during a pack hunt, which ultimately caused her death, his daughter followed a similar fate. Falling from a tree right here in the park and dying from her injuries."

The center of Joss's body went cold as he listened to his failures. He'd been unable to save Marianne from the infection that ravaged her within a short time. And then little Leah, who'd loved to climb trees, had slipped and fallen while he'd been a few yards away having a meeting with the elders in the paddock.

Sid leaned down to Jeanie's ear. Joss knew he wasn't done, yet. There was still one more thing, one more horrible thing.

Sid spoke loudly in Jeanie's ear. "He killed his own son. Broke his neck. Just… snuffed him out and didn't even say goodbye or fuck you or I'm sorry."

The words were a punch to the gut. Joss stared at Jeanie, seeing the emotion flicker in her eyes, from curiosity to disbelief to…. there it was, the feeling he didn't want to see from her—disgust.

Joss's heart cracked.

He should have told her.

"If you're challenging me," Joss said, letting out his claws and fangs, "then challenge *me*. But when I win, don't expect mercy."

"This is a battle for alpha," Amos said, lifting his hand for quiet from the pack, attempting to take over the role of overseeing the challenge.

"Shut. Up." Joss shot a dark look to the male. "You're next."

Amos, who was in his early seventies, blanched, taking a step back from Joss. Joss was so furious he could have breathed fire.

With a rage-filled roar, he launched himself at his brother. One way or another, only one of them would be standing at the end of the battle.

Jeanie was a flurry of emotion that was capped off with a blistering amount of pain. For some reason, Sid liked grabbing her by her hair. When she was a kid, someone had pulled her hair and it hurt. But not like this, which was a pain level approaching nuclear.

She'd known his mate and daughter had died, but he'd never told her how he lost his son.

Had Joss really killed his son?

She wouldn't have thought so, but she'd seen the look in Joss's eyes when Sid had spilled the beans. He'd looked so guilty.

Damn she was pissed at Sid. Who blabbed that kind of thing in public?

She knew for sure that if Joss had to do something so terrible, that he'd had no choice. She really couldn't judge him by human standards because wolves had their own laws and behavior. She could tell by the look in his eyes that he hadn't wanted her to find out this way, and that he would have told her if she would've been able to handle it. Knowing him, he was probably worried she'd balk and split.

But she wasn't going anywhere now.

Joss told one of the elders to shut up, bringing her attention back from the pain in her scalp and her spinning mind.

Then Joss bolted across the distance between them with claws on his fingertips and fangs glinting in the firelight. Sid dropped his grip on Jeanie and met Joss, growls and snarls echoing in the night as the two fought for their lives.

Jeanie fell backward but was caught around the neck by one of Sid's pals. He pulled her roughly to her feet and squeezed her throat, baring his fangs. "I don't fuck humans."

Was he serious?

"Good," she said, the word muffled by the gag.

He gave her a menacing look. The pressure on her throat tightened and she gasped, struggling to breathe.

He was going to kill her while Joss was distracted.

Which pissed her off good. How dare this jerk try to take

her away from her soulmate while she was tied up and help-less. Except she didn't really feel helpless. She felt like there was power within her she just hadn't tapped into yet.

Suddenly she wished she'd taken a self-defense class.

Then she knew the power she wielded. She'd been reading the pack's history and law books with Joss earlier that day. They'd discussed what it meant for her as his soul-mate, that she was already the alpha female—even before the ceremony they'd been about to perform. He'd told her it was a tradition, that the ceremony itself wasn't where her power over the pack as alpha female came from, it was their bond as soulmates.

She was alpha female. Right this minute.

And there was a man putting his hands on her, trying to kill her. Until the battle between Joss and Sid was over and a winner was declared, she was still alpha female and that meant something.

Her vision winked out for a moment and she knew she had to act. She slammed her knee upward into the man's crotch. He let go of her with a howl, dropping to his knees. Jeanie reached her bound hands up for the gag and pulled it from her mouth, yanking out hair as she freed herself.

Desiree and the other man started toward Jeanie, but she rolled to her knees and rose unsteadily to her feet.

"I'm alpha female!" she shouted. "Protectors!"

For a moment, no one moved. The pack was watching the battle and not her. Desiree and the man both smirked and Jeanie's heart fell. She shook her head. No, she'd read the laws correctly.

"I'm Joss's soulmate and that makes me alpha female, period. Protectors, take those who stood against my mate into custody or face Joss's wrath when he defeats Sid and continues his rightful place as alpha." She straightened her shoulders and raised her voice, the sound carrying over the melee and reaching the pack members. In moments, Desiree, the two men with her, and Amos the elder were held by a handful of pack members. Anke and Jess raced to Jeanie, pulling her away from the battle and helping to free her wrists.

"Doc!" Anke yelled.

A woman appeared with a bag in her hand. "I'm Paula, the pack doctor."

Jeanie put her hand up. "I don't need help right now."

"You're bleeding," Paula said. "Can you even see out of that eye?"

"Joss first, then me."

"As you wish, Alpha," Paula said, giving her a stern look that was part disapproving parent and part pride.

"I'm glad you figured it out," Jess said.

"I wish someone could have clued me in earlier." Jeanie rubbed her wrists which were torn and bloodied from the rough rope. Her entire body ached, but she couldn't worry about that with Joss fighting for both their lives.

"We're not allowed to interfere," Paula said. "But we can't ignore a direct order from the alpha, either."

"We didn't know if Joss had told you that you could ask for help," Anke said. "I wanted to go to you, but my mate wouldn't let me, he was afraid I'd be hurt in the process."

"I understand, I'm not angry. I just wish I'd remembered what Joss told me earlier."

She turned her attention to the brawl. Both males were bloodied, fists flying, with loud growls filling the air. She wanted her mate to win. Not just because she thought he was the rightful alpha of the pack but because their lives had just gotten started and she wasn't ready to say goodbye.

Plus if he lost, she was pretty damn sure that Sid would kill her.

She closed her eyes and touched the part of her that felt

connected to Joss. She wasn't a wolf, but she was a wolf's soulmate. As alien as everything happening was to her, she knew in her heart that she and Joss were meant to find each other, and she wasn't about to let tonight be their last night on earth.

Focusing all her thoughts on her feelings for him, she opened her eyes and watched.

You're the sexiest guy I've ever met, Joss. Full of life, and so damn powerful. I've never met your equal, and certainly this poser has no business usurping your rightful position. I know you won't fail because you're the best man for the job. The best man for me.

I love you. So much.

Come back to me.

CHAPTER FIFTEEN

Joss's brain rattled in his skull, his teeth clacking together as Sid punched him in the jaw. Stars exploded in his vision and he staggered back, dropping to one knee. He wanted to shift and tear his brother apart, but it was against the alpha challenge rules. Twenty years ago, the fight had been over faster. Joss wasn't an old man by any stretch, but he wasn't in his twenties anymore, either.

What kept Joss going was knowing that Jeanie's life was on the line, too.

He heard her ask for help from the Protectors, the pack's designated warriors, and pride filled him. She'd risen up against the fear that he'd felt through their connection, and she'd remembered what he'd told her. She wasn't alone. As long as he was alpha, she was alpha female, and that still meant something.

Joss swiveled on his feet, narrowly missing a blow from Sid. Joss shoved hard against Sid's back, using his momentum against him. Sid hit the ground with a dull thud and Joss was on top of him, cranking an arm behind him and shoving his face into the ground. He felt Jeanie's emotions flood through him—all her love and hope directed at him, almost like he could read her thoughts.

Sid struggled under Joss, but the battle was over.

Joss raised his head and found Jeanie standing with the pack. She was wounded but valiant.

If he let Sid live, they'd forever be watching their backs, wondering when he'd strike again. For sure he would. This was a male who'd let darkness override everything good about him. He wasn't even Joss's brother anymore, simply a shell of the male he'd once been.

With a howl that reverberated from deep within him, Joss snapped Sid's neck, ending his life.

The four who'd stood with Sid against Joss fell dead to the ground at the hands of the Protectors, who then took a knee with the pack.

Joss rose to his feet, never taking his eyes off Jeanie. She remained standing, her eyes shining with unshed tears. Striding to her, he searched her face for signs of her disgust at what he'd done but found only love. He was afraid to hurt her if he touched her, but she didn't seem to care, pulling him close and hugging him.

He dropped his face to her neck and inhaled her sweet scent. "I'm sorry."

"For what?" she asked.

She leaned back in his arms and gave him a smile that made her already bloody lip crack and bleed fresh.

"Are you serious? I kept things from you. And to top it all off, you're injured."

"So are you. Don't be sorry about anything. I figured out who I am tonight."

"Oh?"

"Your soulmate. And a kickass alpha female."

He chuckled, his chest aching from what he was certain were cracked ribs. "Damn straight."

Turning to face the pack, Joss kept Jeanie close to his side. The two elders who hadn't known about Amos's betrayal joined the couple.

Joss looked at them and nodded.

Mel, the oldest of all the elders, spoke with a loud voice, "Tonight we begin a new chapter. Our alpha has proven himself once more to be able to handle any threat. Jeanie didn't back down in the face of danger but stood for her soulmate. They both embody what we should strive for as a pack—honor, loyalty, and strength in the face of adversity. I give you tonight, the new alpha couple—Joss and Jeanie. Mark each other and seal your mating."

Joss looked at his beaten-up soulmate, worried about causing her more pain. She was swaying slightly, her eyes glazing a bit from the pain of her injuries. She seemed to sense his hesitation and she sniffled.

"We came for this tonight," she said with a low voice. Swinging her hair to one side to bare her neck, she moved in front of him, bringing his arms around her body.

The pack watched as Joss looked down at her throat, hearing the steady thump of her pulse. She wasn't scared. He adored that about her. It didn't matter that she couldn't change into an animal like he could. She was strong in her own way, a female to be reckoned with.

"I don't know what I'd do without you," he whispered.

"You don't have to find out," she said.

She brought his hand to her mouth with a curious humming sound, and his body sprang to life. Painful as that was. She snarled softly and he made a mental note to ask her to do that again when they were alone. It was the sexiest sound.

"Love you," he said.

"Love you, too."

They struck at the same time, their blunt teeth digging

into each other's flesh to bruise and symbolically mark. The pack lifted their heads and howled a joyous chorus. Joss lifted from Jeanie's throat and added his howl. Jeanie released her grip on his wrist and yelled, "Woo hoo!"

With a chuckle, Joss turned her in his arms and kissed her gently. "I'm so glad you're safe."

"Trust me, I am too."

"Doc?" Joss said.

Paula rose from her knees as the pack rejoiced in the new alpha pair. "I really need to take you to the infirmary," she said.

"He's worse off than I am," Jeanie said, jerking her head toward Joss.

"He can shift to help speed up his healing, but you don't have that ability."

"I'm not going to shift," Joss said.

Jeanie looked up at him. "Why not?"

"Because I want to heal with you."

"That's dumb, you know." Her scowl softened into a smile. "But very sweet. I don't want to leave right now, we just got mated and the pack's happy."

"Ten minutes," Paula said sternly.

"Twenty and I won't pull rank on you," Jeanie countered.

Joss kissed her temple with a chuckle. "You were born to be alpha female."

"Fine, fine. You two are perfect for each other. Stubborn to the core. Twenty minutes and not a minute more," Paula said.

Joss and Jeanie spent their time meeting with the pack and accepting their congratulations. He'd motioned for the Protectors to dispose of the bodies, and they did, stealing them away to the far corner of the paddock, where a fire pit would be dug and the bodies burned until nothing remained. He'd take a turn watching over the dead once he got Jeanie into the infirmary and her wounds tended. She kept telling him she was fine, but he could see, now that the adrenaline had ebbed, that she was feeling all the injuries.

He wanted to bring all those assholes back to life and kill them all over again.

After they'd made the rounds of the entire pack, Joss left them to the party and carried Jeanie to the maintenance shed. Anke, Zeger, Auden, Jess, and Paula followed him, Auden grabbing the door hidden in the floor ahead of them. Once they were inside the infirmary, Joss set Jeanie on a hospital bed and took a step away to let Paula tend to her.

"Where are you going?" Jeanie asked.

"Nowhere, love," he said. "Just letting the most important female in my life get taken care of first."

"Anyone who can't see these two naked needs to take off," Paula said. "I've got exams to give."

"We'll be outside if you need us," Auden said.

"We're so glad you're both okay," Jess said.

"Thanks for standing with me," Jeanie said, grumbling at Paula as she tugged her sandals off her dirty, bloody feet.

"It's our honor," Zeger said.

The foursome stepped out of the room and shut the door, and Joss looked down at Jeanie as Paula helped her stand. "Let's get you cleaned up, and then I can properly tend the wounds. Alpha?"

Joss picked up Jeanie and carried her into the small bathroom where a stand-up shower waited. He set Jeanie gently on the floor and turned on the water, testing it with his hand while he kept her close.

"I want to cry," she said into his chest.

"Go ahead. You deserve a good cry after what you endured."

"I'm trying to be strong."

He tilted her face up. "Crying doesn't make you weak. You happen to be the strongest female I've ever known."

"I didn't fight back."

He scoffed. "Yes you did."

She shook her head, tears splashing on her cheeks. "I called for help. If the pack hadn't decided to help me, then I don't know what would have happened."

His wolf snarled unhappily. How could she think she wasn't strong? She'd shown herself to be the epitome of the word. "You used the Protectors for what their purpose is. That's not weak, it's smart. You were caught off guard by the attack and outnumbered, and aside from those two things, you're also human. Shifters naturally possess more strength."

Her mouth turned down, her eyes filling with tears. "How can I be a leader of people who could kill me so easily?"

"Because you were born for this, love. I promise. My... former brother, and those who followed him, aren't typical of our kind. I'd never think of using a mate—human or otherwise—to hurt someone else. It's a bitch move."

She chuckled a little. He brushed the tears from her cheeks.

"Listen, I failed miserably to protect you. Your injuries and the scent of your blood is making my wolf want to go on the warpath."

"You didn't fail. How could you know that woman was spying on his behalf?"

"Exactly." He tweaked her chin. "I've been a wolf my entire life. I've never known a situation like what happened tonight to have ever occurred. If I couldn't anticipate a retaliatory move like this, how could you?"

She leaned into him, hugging him tightly. "You're saying I shouldn't beat myself up because they already did?"

His upper lip curled. "Yes."

"I still kinda want to cry."

"Your adrenaline is gone, you're safe. It's okay to feel relieved by that."

"You're pretty sweet, Joss." She went onto her toes and kissed him.

"Just for you."

He helped her out of her dress then stripped himself, ducking under the spray and turning the shower head until it was a soft mist and not hard needles of water pounding his skin. She joined him, and together they gently washed each other, cleaning the dirt and dried blood from their skin and cataloging their injuries. Once out of the shower, she wrapped a towel around her hair and dried her body, then donned the hospital gown he pulled from a cabinet for her. He found a pair of scrub pants and put them on.

Jeanie sat on the bed, and Paula checked her over, while Joss kept a watchful eye on the exam.

"Is Sarah going to be okay?" Jeanie asked.

"Yes. She's banged up a bit, but she shifted to heal her injuries. The tumble down the stairs could have killed her, so she's thankful to be alive," Paula said as she bandaged Jeanie's wrists.

"What's the verdict?" Joss asked, when the doctor had finished her exam and tending to Jeanie's wounds.

"Nothing too serious, fortunately." She walked to a medicine cabinet and removed a small bottle. Then she filled a cup with water and brought both over to them. "Keep an ice pack on the eye, it'll heal in a few days. I put ointment on the lip, you can apply it every few hours to help promote healing. The wrists are bruised and scratched, keep the bandages on for a day. The biggest issue is the bruise on the stomach, but nothing inside is affected, just the skin." She handed two white pills to Jeanie and the water. "Pain pills. They'll knock you out. You can take one every six to eight hours. The best thing is rest."

Paula handed the bottle to Joss. "Thanks," he said.

"Now for you," Paula said.

"I'm fine."

"That bruise on your side begs to differ," Paula said.

"I had to get checked out," Jeanie said when she'd popped the pills and drained the cup. "All's fair."

He snorted. "Even without shifting I have accelerated healing. I'll be fine. There's nothing to be done for the cracked ribs anyway. They just have to heal."

"You should shift," Jeanie said.

"Not a chance."

"Stubborn man," she said, narrowing her eyes but giving him a secret smile.

"It's what makes me a great alpha."

Paula shook her head with a chuckle. "If you need me, holler. I won't offer you pain meds because I know you won't take them, but you can take two if you want."

He put the bottle in the pocket of the scrubs, then lifted Jeanie into his arms. "Thank you."

"It's what I'm here for."

Joss carried Jeanie to their home and laid her in bed. She yawned and gave him a sleepy smile. He fetched an ice pack from the freezer and wrapped it in a kitchen towel. He put it in her hand, and she laid it gently on her eye.

"Why did Paula say you wouldn't take the pain pills?"

"Because they mess with my wolf's ability to be alert. I'd sleep too deeply, and it would make me feel unsettled."

"Can I ask you about something that was said at the challenge?"

He sat on the edge of the bed and stifled a weary sigh. "You want to know about my children."

"How old was your daughter when she died?"

He nodded and rubbed the space over his heart. "Leah was ten. When Marianne died after a lengthy battle with infection, Leah and Jesse were distraught and they needed me. I was too wrapped up in my own grief to be a good parent and I threw myself into being alpha. I left them with pack members while I spent days in meetings with the council, doing anything to numb the pain of Marianne's loss. Jesse grew colder as the months went by, but Leah was a happy little girl for the most part, especially when she was climbing a big, old tree in the paddock. I was having a meeting with the elders and she was doing what she always did—climbing that tree. It had rained recently, and the bark was loose on some of the upper branches. She slipped and fell, dying instantly." It still replayed in his mind sometimes, hearing the crunch of the bark as it slipped from under her feet and her screaming. He'd raced for her but hadn't been able to get to her before she fell.

"I'm so sorry."

He grimaced, remembering how angry he'd been about everything. He'd chopped down the tree, spending hours and hours hacking away at it, digging into the ground and pulling the roots out. He'd never wanted to see it again because it was a reminder that he was a terrible father.

"I overreacted to what happened to Leah by paying even closer attention to Jesse. He was twelve when she died, and by that time, though, he was emotionally distant from everyone, hardened and turning ruthless. He only got worse as time went on."

"Is what Sid said true? Did you kill him?"

"Yes. I want to say I didn't have a choice, but the truth is that as alpha, there's always a choice." He scrubbed a hand through his hair, a little bit of worry biting at his neck that Jeanie might think him a monster for what he'd done. But she's already heard the news in the worst of ways, and he would never lie to her. "Jesse was a loud-mouthed trouble-maker. He had a sweet side when he was a kid, but after losing his mother and sister, that part of him died. He had a wolves-rule mindset. He'd go out of his way to torment someone he didn't like. No matter how often I spoke to him about his behavior, he was never sorry. I don't think he was ever going to be suited to be alpha, he was too volatile.

"A year before we started the VIP tours, Jesse was out with some pack members at a bar. A group of the gorillas was there as well, celebrating the birthday of one of the males. From what we heard about the incident, a human female offered to give the gorilla a kiss, and Jesse demanded he get one as well. When she refused, Jesse and his cronies got aggressive. Human bouncers stepped in, and Jesse and the wolves overpowered the humans and caused a lot of damage to the bar. The gorillas put a stop to the fighting, paid the owner for the damages, and got the wolves out. The wolves were punished for starting a small riot in a human business by not being allowed to shift on the next full moon."

"That's bad?" she asked.

"It makes us feel like something's missing if we can't shift on the full moon." Joss stopped speaking for a moment and Jeanie touched his hand. He brought it to his lips and kissed her knuckles. "Jesse held a grudge against the gorillas after that. When we started the VIP tours, Jesse was a guide. For the most part he did well, although he could be aggressive with the human females, mocking or teasing them in a way that sounded innocent but wasn't. At any rate, Zane, one of the gorillas, found his soulmate in a VIP patron. Jesse knew that she was Zane's soulmate and—in full view of Zane in his shifted form and the rest of the gorillas—tried to hurt the female. Zane ripped the fence apart and rescued her. She passed out in fear, of course, and Zane carried her into the paddock and down to their private area to recover."

Jeanie sucked in a sharp breath. "Was she okay?"

"Yes. Just freaked out."

"What happened?"

"We have cameras on each Jeep in the tour, so we got the footage and showed the alphas. Jesse broke three of our laws, and the sentence was to wear a special collar called a Flayer, which prevents shifting, for three years—one year for each broken law. Not shifting on the full moon makes our wolves crazy. We can get away with it if we're regularly shifting like for the VIP tours, but the rules of the Flayer state that the wolf in question can't leave their home for any reason. He was effectively under house arrest for three years—no shifting, no communing with the pack, and no finding out if a human coming into the park for a VIP tour was his soulmate."

"It sounds like a terrible punishment."

"It would be hell," Joss agreed. "It should have been over. Jesse should have accepted his punishment and ridden it out. Instead, he snuck into the security office and took the footage of the attack, then edited it so that it appeared as if Zane attacked Adriana, and Jesse was a victim. Then he leaked it to the human media."

"Oh!" Jeanie said. "I remember hearing about that. I had no idea it was this park, though. How awful! What did Jesse hope to accomplish?"

"He wanted to make Zane pay."

"I don't understand."

"If the human authorities believed that a natural gorilla had broken through the security fence, attacked a tour guide, and kidnapped a guest, they could demand that gorilla be killed. Or removed from the park. We don't have any natural gorillas here to put in place of our shifters. It was terribly dangerous for all of us. We do have laws that, if broken, will result in death. One of them is purposely causing our people to come under investigation by humans in any way.

"I want to say I had a choice. That I could have let Jesse

live and simply found another way to deal with the fallout, but the truth was that I couldn't. I couldn't justify letting him live when he was a danger to all of us. It was the hardest, worst thing I ever did, and I didn't think I'd survive it myself. He was defiant to the very end. I think... he wanted me to kill him. The Flayer was too much of a punishment for him to endure, and he wanted to cause as much trouble for our people as he could on his way out of this life."

"You said it's tough to be an alpha. This sounds like a prime example."

"Indeed."

She sat up, wincing a little, and hugged him. "I'm sorry he put you in the position to carry out the punishment."

"Me too, sweetheart."

"Was the park okay after that? What happened with the media?"

"As part of the alphas' damage control, the news media was told that Adriana wasn't harmed, and neither were the guide and driver. The cover story was that Adriana had been working closely with the gorillas for months, and the footage had been altered by the guide in retaliation for not getting a salary increase. We invited the media to the park to show them that Adriana was fine. She was in the gorilla paddock acting as a zookeeper. We had Jasper, one of the pack, stand in for Jesse who looked similar enough to pass for him. Jasper explained that he faked the dash-cam footage and apologized for the ruse, and then Adriana spoke to the reporters about what happened. It seemed to appease everyone, and we were fined for the broken fence, but otherwise we didn't have problems."

"It would have been awful if his actions had led to the shifter secret being discovered."

"Exactly."

She settled back on the mattress and was quiet for a long

moment. "I don't understand everything you deal with as alpha, but I can see why you had no choice. He was dangerous and you had so many people to think about. I'm sorry you went through it. And I'm sorry that Sid tried to use what caused you grief against you to hurt me."

He bit back a snarl at the mention of his brother. Shaking his head, he said, "So much loss."

"We just need to move on. I'm safe, you're safe, the pack is safe." She gave him a sleepy smile, the pain meds clearly kicking in. "I don't think less of you for what you went through. I think you're the strongest person I've ever known, and I don't just mean physical strength. You're alpha for a reason. You make the hard choices."

"I'm sorry I didn't tell you before. My brother should never have had the chance to use that against me."

"I understand why you didn't. You wondered what I'd think of you, or if I might leave you."

"Exactly."

"I can't think of anything that would make me walk away from you, Joss. You're everything to me, and you've got my heart."

"You have mine, too." He leaned over and kissed her gently, mindful of her injuries. "Thank you for caring enough about me to hear me out."

"Of course." She stifled a yawn and closed her eyes. "Will you stay with me?"

"First I need to check on things in the paddock, I'll be about a half hour. I've got Protectors coming to stand guard outside. I don't want you to be afraid of anything."

"The bad guys are all gone. You put down the threat. I'm the least scared person around."

"I love you, Jeanie." He stood and looked down at his beautiful soulmate. "I'll be right back."

"I'll be right here. Alpha." Her voice slurred at the end,

and she fell asleep. He watched her for a moment, his wolf of a mind to stay right there and keep watch over her. But duty called, and he needed to ensure his people were taking care of things.

Giving one last look at his sleeping beauty, he strode from the bedroom and closed the door silently behind him. Outside the house, he spoke to the Protectors who were going to keep watch. Although he didn't think there was any danger to be had now that everyone involved with his brother was dead, for his own peace of mind he wanted extra eyes on his soulmate. His wolf wouldn't be happy until he was back with Jeanie.

Back with the female who held his heart firmly in her hands.

CHAPTER SIXTEEN

J eanie smiled from behind the omelet station in the marketplace. The man holding out his plate had an eager gleam in his eyes. The line for the newly established omelet station was very long, and she couldn't help but love how much the shifters enjoyed her cooking. When she'd first become the alpha female of the pack, she'd spent two weeks getting to know the pack members. She'd never know what it was like to be a shifter, but she could still be a great leader with Joss at her side.

And then she'd gotten antsy. Joss worked in the finance office and handled a lot of day-to-day park operations. She couldn't ask him to hang out with her all the time, and she hated when they couldn't be together as much as they both wanted for one reason or another. So she'd asked him to help her find something to do within the park that wouldn't make his wolf crazy. It was out of the question for her to be topside in the park while he was underground in the offices.

She'd been in the marketplace having breakfast with Anke and Jess when someone complained that there weren't enough cooks for the breakfast rush. Jeanie offered to help and had really enjoyed getting back to cooking. That day, Marcus asked her if she'd like to take over the breakfast shift and be the team leader, and she'd jumped at the chance.

The first thing she'd done was get an omelet station set up, and it was the most popular station for breakfast.

She flipped the omelet that was stuffed with four different meats and a ton of cheese. "August, right?" she asked the big guy across from her.

There were so many shifters in the park she thought it would take forever for her to learn all their names, but working in the marketplace was helping her get to know those outside of the pack. There were many omelet station regulars, and the gorilla shifter was one of them.

"Yep. How's your morning going?" He flashed her a smile and dropped his gaze to the sizzling pan.

"Busy, but that's the way I like it. Yours?"

"Better once I get an omelet."

She checked the omelet, topped it with a bit more cheese, and then slid it onto his waiting plate.

"Thanks, Jeanie."

"Enjoy!"

The next male in line greeted her and gave his order, and she got to work. Ninety minutes later the breakfast rush was over, and Jeanie was able to take a break. She grabbed her favorite metal water bottle with a painted picture of a wolf on it and went to find Joss.

She knocked on the open door and he looked up, smiling with a soft growl when he met her gaze.

"Hello, sweetheart," he said.

She walked behind the desk and bent to give him a kiss, and he pulled her into his lap. She giggled and kissed him more fully, then set the water bottle on the desk. Running her fingers through his hair, she said, "Hi to you, too."

"You smell like breakfast meats. I could eat you up."

"Lemme shut the door." She wiggled her brows, and he barked out a laugh.

"Such a tempting vixen." He rested his forehead against hers. "We'll have to wait until lunch to fool around. Unfortunately I have to go meet with the construction company for a walk-through of the apartment complex."

"Can I join you?"

"I'd love the company."

She kissed on him a bit more and climbed off his lap. They walked through the offices and up into the employee cafeteria. A golf cart with the park's logo on the front was waiting outside, driven by Jupiter. In the passenger seat, Caesar, the lion alpha, turned and greeted them.

"Nice to see you again, Jeanie," Caesar said.

"You too."

Joss put his arm around her as the cart jerked into motion. They followed a maintenance path to the back of the park, where an apartment complex was nearing completion.

"How many apartments are there?" Jeanie asked as the building came into view.

"Eight," Joss answered. "Two stories with four apartments on each floor."

The small complex was within the park. It was accessible inside the park by the maintenance path which led to a security gate. Outside the park, there was a hidden drive that lead to another gate. The complex was surrounded by a tall security fence. Jupiter entered a code and the gate rumbled to life and opened. Once inside, Jupiter parked next to trucks and vans that sported a business logo—Dexter Construction.

"Are these guys like you?" Jeanie asked.

"No," Joss said. He leaned in and whispered in her ear, "They're human."

"You've got employees in the park who like to build things," she said. She climbed out of the cart and took Joss's hand, shielding her eyes from the morning sun to look at the building.

Caesar said, "We couldn't spare them for such a large project."

"That makes sense," Jeanie said.

"Good morning," a tall man with graying hair said as he walked around one of the construction company vehicles.

"Morning," Caesar said, shaking his hand.

"This is my wife, Jeanie," Joss said after shaking his hand. "This is Dexter, he's the owner."

Jeanie always smiled when Joss referred to her as his wife. They were planning to get married officially at some point, but whenever they were in public, he called her his wife instead of mate.

Dexter led their group through the complex, explaining the work that needed to be completed. Jeanie trailed behind, enjoying the peeks into each apartment. The apartments were for the human mates who had family that would find it odd if they weren't able to come visit them where they lived. If she had any family still alive, she was sure they'd think it was weird that she was living and working at the park but wouldn't be able to let them visit.

"It looks good," Joss said, standing outside the eighth apartment and leaning against the rail.

"Thanks," Dexter said. "We're still on-track to be finished in November. You've got floor guys you want to use, or do you want us to handle that?"

"We'd like you to deal with it," Caesar said. "That way we don't have to contract with anyone else."

"Sounds good. When we're ready for that, we've got sample books that you can pick from."

The group moved on to inspect the exterior of the building. Joss moved until he was caging Jeanie against the rail and gave her a kiss.

"You like the apartments?" he asked.

"Yes. They're a good idea."

"Indeed. I'm glad you and I don't have to put on a charade to use one, even though I'm sad I didn't get a chance to meet your parents, or for you to meet mine."

"Would they have liked me, considering I'm not like you?"

"My mom, yes. My dad was pretty traditional." Joss blew out a breath. "I'm not sure if he would like what we're doing with the VIP tours or how much our people are changing. I want to say that he would have changed with the times—I sure have—but it's hard to say."

"You've changed with the times?" she asked, arching a brow.

"Are you kidding, sweetheart? A few years ago I'd have kicked out one of my people for being with one of yours. I was raised with the notion that purity of our people was the only way to keep things going. The tours—seeing how happy people are with their one right person no matter what they can or can't change into—it's changed me. And then there's you." He tucked a lock of hair behind her ear and she shivered at the light touch. "You've changed me in a thousand ways just by being you. I'm happier than ever, happier than I deserve to be, and I feel like I can be a more effective leader."

"You deserve to be happy, Joss." She cupped his face and smiled at him. Such a sexy male, and all hers. She felt supremely lucky.

"I have an idea," Joss said, his voice dropping low in a way that made her insides feel all warm and melty.

"Do tell."

"Let's take the rest of the day off."

"That's the best idea I've heard all day."

He smiled and kissed her with a nearly imperceptible growl. "I'm all about good ideas when it comes to you, sweetheart."

"Lead the way."

They checked in with the others so Joss could sign off on the building's progress, and then they opted to walk back to the employee cafeteria together instead of waiting for the golf cart. She loved strolling through the park, seeing the happy families and hearing the laughter all around them. The Amazing Adventures Safari Park was an incredible place, and she was glad to be part of it. Even if humans didn't know how special the place really was, she was glad she knew. Glad that her neighbor had given her the tour ticket so she could meet the most amazing guy on the planet. How different her life was, because she'd stepped out on a limb and tried something new.

Who could have guessed that going to the park would change her life so significantly?

When they were safely in the wolves' private living area, Joss lifted her into his arms and carried her swiftly to their home, where they spent the day reveling in each other's love. She'd never get enough of the gruff, sexy male who made her knees weak and her heart pound in anticipation. He was everything to her, and she knew all the way to the center of her being that she was everything to him, too.

And it was all thanks to a VIP tour ticket.

AVAILABLE NOW IN THE WERE ZOO SERIES

Neo (Were Zoo Book Ten)

www.rebutlerauthor.com

CONTACT THE AUTHOR

Website: http://www.rebutlerauthor.com
Email: rebutlerauthor@gmail.com
Facebook: www.facebook.com/R.E.ButlerAuthorPage

ALSO FROM R. E. BUTLER

Tempting Treasure
Having Hope

Hyena Heat
Every Night Forever
Every Dawn Forever
Every Sunset Forever
Every Blissful Moment
Every Heavenly Moment
Every Miraculous Moment
Every Angelic Moment

The Necklace Chronicles
The Tribe's Bride
The Gigolo's Bride
The Tiger's Bride
The Alpha Wolf's Mate
The Jaguar's Bride
The Author's True Mate

Norlanian Brides
Paoli's Bride
Warrick's Bride
Dex's Bride
Norlanian Brides Volume One
Villi's Bride
Dero's Bride

Saber Chronicles
Saber Chronicles Volume One (Books One - Four)

Sable Cove
Must Love Familiars

Tails
Memory
Mercy
Emberly
AnnaRose

Uncontrollable Shift
The Alpha's Christmas Mate
The Dragon's Treasured Mate
The Bear's Reluctant Mate
The Leopard Twins' Christmas Mate

Vampire Beloved
Want
Need
Ache

Were Zoo
Zane
Jupiter
Win
Justus
Devlin
Kelley
Auden
Tayme
Joss
Neo

Wiccan-Were-Bear
A Curve of Claw
A Flash of Fang
A Price for a Princess
A Bond of Brothers

A Bead of Blood
A Twitch of Tail
A Promise on White Wings
A Slash of Savagery
Awaken a Wolf
Daeton's Journey
A Dragon for December
A Muse for Mishka
The Wiccan-Were-Bear Series Volume One
The Wiccan-Were-Bear Series Volume Two
The Wiccan-Were-Bear Series Volume Three
A Wish for Their Woman

Wilde Creek
Volume One (Books 1 and 2)
Volume Two (Books 3 and 4)
Volume Three (Books 5 and 6)
The Hunter's Heart (Book Seven)
The Beta's Heart (Book Eight)

The Wolf's Mate
The Wolf's Mate Book 1: Jason & Cadence
The Wolf's Mate Book 2: Linus & The Angel
The Wolf's Mate Book 3: Callie & The Cats
The Wolf's Mate Book 4: Michael & Shyne
The Wolf's Mate Book 5: Bo & Reika
The Wolf's Mate Book 6: Logan & Jenna
The Wolf's Mate Book 7: Lindy & The Wulfen

Available now in the Were Zoo Series: Neo (Book Ten)

Gorilla shifter Neo feels like he's been waiting for his soulmate forever, even though he's only twenty-six. He keeps himself busy during the day working on the Amazing Adventures Safari Park vehicles, where he and his fellow shifters live in secrecy from humans. But the lonely nights are getting to him, and he wonders when he'll meet the other half of his heart.

Danielle Fitzgerald knows her stepfather Dexter and his son Khyle are keeping something from her and her mother, but she can't figure out what it is. There's something off about both of them, and the group of men that work for their construction company. Against her dad's wishes, she takes a VIP ticket for the safari tour, and finds herself entranced with one of the gorillas.

Neo knows the moment that the vehicle with his soulmate stops in front of the gorilla paddock and his beast can't wait to meet her. He knows it will take a while before he can share the truth of his shift with her, but what he doesn't count on is her stepfamily's secret. When the truth comes out, will Dani be able to stay with Neo at the park, or will her family steal her away before he can stop them?

Printed in Great Britain
by Amazon